OUT OF HERE

A SENIOR CLASS YEARBOOK
OUT OF HERE

SANDY ASHER

LODESTAR BOOKS
Dutton   New York

Library of Congress Cataloging-in-Publication Data
Asher, Sandy.
    Out of here: a senior class yearbook / by Sandy Asher.—1st ed.
    p. cm.
    Summary: The lives of Stacey Lawrence and other seniors at Oakview High School in Eli, Missouri, are interconnected in sometimes unseen ways as they move from the first day of school to graduation day.
    ISBN 0-525-67418-7
    [1. High schools—Fiction. 2. Schools—Fiction. 3. Interpersonal relations—Fiction.] I. Title.
PZ7.A8160u 1993 [Fic]—dc20   92-35188
                                                                    CIP
                                                                    AC

Published in the United States by Lodestar Books,
an affiliate of Dutton Children's Books,
a division of Penguin Books USA Inc.,
375 Hudson Street, New York, New York 10014

Published simultaneously in Canada
by McClelland & Stewart, Toronto

Editor: Virginia Buckley   Designer: Richard Granald

Printed in the U.S.A.   First Edition   10 9 8 7 6 5 4 3 2

for Harvey

CONTENTS

This feeling of solitary helplessness lends support to the theory that nightmares go back to a very primitive period of mankind's mental life, to a time when we were indeed helpless, alone, and surrounded by incomprehensible but very vivid dangers.

—Robert Wernick,
Smithsonian, March 1989

In other words, high school . . .

—Walt Hightower,
Valedictorian
Eighty-eighth graduating class
Oakview Senior High

FALL

OUT OF HERE

Don't close the doors, Stacey Lawrence thought. Just leave them open, okay? Do that much for me, and maybe I'll be able to handle the rest.

Shoulders, book bags, and elbows propelled her through the entrance to Oakview High School and past the principal's office, already packed with lost souls. Shifting her notebook and purse to one arm, she unglued a strand of damp, dark hair from her cheek with her free hand and pushed it behind her ear. September in Eli, Missouri: The heat and humidity were already brutal at eight-thirty in the morning, and Oakview was not air-conditioned. Ceiling fans would keep the odors of hair spray, armpits, and stale cigarette smoke mingling in her nostrils all day.

"Taylor! Hey, man! How's it going, Liver Lips?"

"Melanie! I can't be-leeeeve it! Your *hair!*"

Stacey turned to look back at the double doors one last time and glimpsed a sliver of summer light over the silhouettes gyrating behind her. They'll close them, she told herself. They always do. For security reasons, she supposed. Instead of feeling safe, she fought off a tremor of claustrophobia.

The crowd jostled her down the hall. Someone stomped on her toe; someone else popped a wad of gum next to her ear. A huddle at the foot of the north stairs blocked her way up to the second floor.

I am *not* here, she thought, edging around the blockade. I'm not doing any of this. I *think* I am, but I'm really not.

At last, she was facing her assigned locker, outside Room 209. She pulled the combination lock out of her purse and hooked it into the locker handle, then squeezed

2

until its thick metal lumps and edges hurt her hand. This is a dream, she decided, and closed her eyes. I'll wake up, and it'll be gone.

"Stacey! Hi! How was your summer?"

Stacey's eyes flew open, and she grabbed the loose-leaf notebook slipping from the crook of her arm. "Hi, Lee!" she called to the pretty blonde grinning at her. Heads bobbed between them like clouds crossing the sun. "It was terrific! I was—"

"Great!" Lee broke in. Dismissing Stacey with a wave of her hand, she shouted a greeting to someone else, farther down the hall.

Stacey felt the doors closing, like a pressure on her temples and inside her lungs, pinning her down, locking her in. She watched Lee Whitaker sail away, her usual hangers-on moving with her like a protective flotilla.

One small vessel broke off and stayed with Stacey. "The missing link!" Nicole Drake cried. "I must've called your house a million times. I thought you'd moved away or died or something."

Returning the eager smile in front of her, Stacey gave Nicole a hug with her free arm. "We just got back last night," she explained. "The car broke down in Nowhere, Illinois—a carbon copy of Eli, by the way, except we're surrounded by cows and they've got corn. What they *didn't* have was the part we needed, so we had to hole up in the local Bates Motel."

"Your dad must have been fuming!"

"He's been fuming all summer. My sister-in-law kept threatening to hose him down—"

"Never mind them," Nicole broke in. "What about me? I've had exactly two postcards from you since June. I wrote you all about my fabulous adventures—Burger Chef, the mall. Lee's folks put in a pool—that was a highlight. And all I got back was 'Nicole, Can't wait to tell you all about it. Stay cool. Love, Stacey.' What's the good of having friends in faraway places if you don't get any mail from them?"

Stacey laughed. Remembering the cards, the tiny village post office, the bright summer mornings so full of promise, she felt her heart leap. "Oh, Nicole, you cannot believe how beautiful it was. And not just the scenery. *Everything.* It was like the whole world opened up for me."

Nicole nodded, but her eyes darted sideways. Stacey followed their lead to the doorway of 208, where Brian Marsh was playfully jabbing at a football player's bicep. Suddenly the player let out a challenging whoop. Brian took off, snaking through the crowd to the end of the hall and around the corner, the player close behind him. People flattened themselves against their lockers to make way.

"He's even better looking with a tan, isn't he?" Nicole said.

"Brian?" Stacey asked. "I guess."

Nicole regarded her with wide eyes. "You guess?"

"Well, he's—he's a kid, Nicole. He's okay for a kid."

"You're a kid," Nicole replied. "I'm a kid. What did you expect him to be—middle-aged? He's a senior, same as us."

But we're not the same, Stacey wanted to tell her. Not anymore. How could she make Nicole understand what she'd seen, what she'd been through, what she *felt?* "The Berkshires—" she stammered. "I—I just—"

"Yah. The Berkshires," Nicole echoed, absently. "Right. So tell me." She edged down the hall, toward the corner where Brian had disappeared.

Stacey tossed her lunch sack into her locker, spun the lock, and fell into step beside Nicole, as she'd done hundreds of times before. Since middle school, the two of them had walked to classes together, sat next to each other at lunch, hung out on weekends together, double-dated, traded clothes and gossip. If you invited Nicole somewhere, you invited Stacey. And vice versa. Sometimes people even mixed them up, but Nicole was the one with the heart-shaped face, her ash blonde hair brushed back from a widow's peak. Stacey was the brunette. Other than that, they were a matched set, two of a kind, best friends.

Stacey took a deep breath. How to do the summer justice? "Tree-covered mountains," she began, sweeping her hand through the air as if to paint the scene for Nicole. "Like giant gods hunched over the lake. Watching, listening. *Alive*. Air so clear and clean, it makes you happy just to breathe it. And in the middle of all this, a theater—actors, audiences, music . . ."

They'd turned the corner. Brian and the football player were nowhere to be seen.

"Ah, nuts," Nicole said. "Well, I've got gym first period. How about you?"

It took Stacey a moment to replace the Berkshires with Oakview. "Computer lab," she recalled at last.

"First lunch?"

"Yes."

"Great."

"I'll finish telling you then, okay? About my summer? Nicole, it was so amazing—"

"Right." Nicole hopped down the first few steps toward the basement, then turned to wave. "See you at lunch. Sit by me."

"Sure," Stacey replied and worked her way into the line headed back up to the third floor.

The warning bell sounded just as she entered the computer room. She took a seat in front of a blank screen and

5

settled her purse and notebook under her chair. Something about that movement, its familiarity, brought the truth crashing in on her: She really was here, in Eli, Missouri, at Oakview High School, on the first day of her senior year.

She was not in the mountains of Massachusetts. Everything she had come to love there, as she had loved nothing else in her entire seventeen and a half years of life, was gone. The theater was dark. The actors had moved on; the audiences, returned home. The mountain gods slept in silence beside the abandoned lake.

There would be next summer. She'd already been promised an apprenticeship. And there would be years and years after that of other theaters, in college and elsewhere. Her life was waiting for her, she assured herself, right there, at the end of this year. Less than a year, really—fall, winter, spring.

Suddenly a hand shot between her face and the computer screen. Fingers wiggled before her eyes, plump fingers tipped with polish the purple of grape ice cones.

"Whaddaya think?" Caroline Beck asked, as a welcome and announcements from the principal's office crackled into the room through the intercom.

Stacey regarded the girl at the next computer. "About what?" she asked. She knew what, of course. The nail polish. But she just couldn't play the game, give the official squeal of approval.

"Passion de Nuit," Caroline replied, in an exaggerated French accent. She wriggled all ten fingers under Stacey's nose. Parts of Caroline were always moving: her mouth, her hips, her enormous boobs. Stacey wondered if she wiggled in her sleep, like vanilla pudding.

At the front of the room, on the far side of several rows of heads and computers, Mr. Ellis waited out the last of

6

the announcements and then launched into his plans for the year. "Personal computer options," he said, "are unlimited. We'll be exploring word processing, database, spreadsheet—"

He opened his arms wide. Enthusiasm made his face shine pink under the fluorescent lights, straight up to his bald head. Can you love computers, Stacey wondered, really *love* them? That would be fine. She wanted everyone to love what they did the way she—

"Wild, huh?" Caroline whispered, nodding at her fingers, then using one Passion de Nuit tip to poke her large, square glasses higher up the bridge of her broad nose.

"Nice," Stacey told her.

Walt Hightower dropped a pile of work sheets at the edge of their table. Stacey smiled a hello at him, then took one stapled set and passed the rest to Caroline.

"I won a free make-over at the mall," Caroline explained.

"Very nice," Stacey said. "And your eye shadow, too. Nice."

At Mr. Ellis's command, the class flipped switches, and computers all over the room hummed to life.

"You don't think it's too much?" Caroline hissed.

Stacey bit her lip. Honesty had been such a big deal at Lakeside Playhouse. The actors evaluated and reevaluated themselves and one another. Directors piled on corrections and suggestions. After long days of rehearsal and performance, everyone had gone over and over scenes, gestures, sentences, phrases, *syllables*, until they were exactly right.

What was the right answer for Caroline? Last year, it would have been "Oh, no, *really*, it's fine." Because Lee's crowd didn't even know Caroline existed, she didn't matter. So what if she looked like grape slush?

In a play, everyone mattered. A weak performance in the smallest part could ruin everything. But could Stacey really tell Caroline she looked like a fool? The right answers were breaking down. Was there one set for school and another for everywhere else?

"Maybe a little bit much," she suggested, trying for the middle ground.

Caroline's mouth fell open. Hurt filled her eyes.

"For school, I mean," Stacey hurried on. "You know, this *dump*. But you look great. Very dramatic."

Caroline grinned. "Thanks," she said.

I'm not going to make it, Stacey told herself. How could she go on discussing nails and lipstick and guys like Brian Marsh when she really, really, *really* did not care about any of that anymore?

Had she ever cared? It seemed that she had sometimes. But other times, she'd felt herself pretending, trying to convince herself that she cared, that she should, that it was important and correct to do so. It had to be because it was to everyone else she knew.

Back then, she'd never even guessed there was a place where other things were far more important. She'd meandered along, making all the right sounds and faces, thinking there was something wrong with her because the sounds so often rang false in her ears and the faces sometimes left the muscles in her jaw aching at the end of the day.

Lee and the others—even Nicole—had accepted what they heard and saw of her. Stacey was the sweet one. Not the clown, not the clone, not the cheerleader, not the creep. Just sweet. Pretty enough in her petite, skinny way; smart enough, but not too smart. She was invited to parties, asked to dance, taken to movies by boys who talked about—nothing much. It had never been quite enough for her, but there had never been anything else. Until this summer.

Mr. Ellis barked out instructions, and Stacey's hands obeyed. She stuck a white label onto a disk, wrote her name across the label in black letters, then slid the disk into its slot. She spelled out her name and the date on the screen and in a workbook. She punched more keys. Directions appeared before her eyes, and she followed them.

But behind her eyes, another path stretched out before her and she followed that one, too—away from the cottage, down the road to tiny Main Street in Lakeside Village, deserted under the noon sun. In the distance, a dog barked and a woman's voice shouted for it to be quiet. Dust rose from the scuffing of her sneakers on the pavement. Nervousness and midday heat matted her T-shirt to her back. An audition. She'd never been to an audition in her life. Her brother was crazy. Why had she listened to him?

Because it was something to do. Something new and different, in a new and different place—where maybe she could be new and different, too. Sweet Stacey. Surely there was more. There had to be more. . . .

Computer lab, math, French. And finally, lunch. Stacey raced to her locker to drop off the morning's books and pick up her lunch, then backtracked to the cafeteria, rising to her toes as she made her way toward Lee's table, searching the crowd around it for Nicole.

Would there be a seat saved for her? How many lunches had begun with that same worry? And here it was again, tightening her stomach muscles far more than hunger ever could. "Sit by me," Nicole had said. But would she remember? Funny how all the old fears came right back, regular as September, the minute those big doors banged shut. What if she had to sit alone?

9

Alone, shadows lengthening around her, she'd watched each new audience make its way up the path to the theater, knowing that soon it would all begin again—the words, the movement, the magic. Imagine *wanting* to be alone, to savor the anticipation! There, alone was fine, full, nothing at all like loneliness. Here, it was unthinkable, even when not being alone was still lonely.

Where was Nicole? Stacey hated having to care that much, but she did. It was something about this place, about those doors, that made her do and say and think and feel the oddest things. Had she or Nicole ever forgotten to save each other a seat? No. But it could happen.

"Stacey! Over here!"

Stacey drew a huge breath of relief as she spotted Nicole waving her on. The double table near the cafeteria line was already mobbed with people. Lee sat midway down one side, her back to the steam tables, a tray already in front of her. Others gathered around with their brown bag lunches, trays, and odd assortments of candy bars, Doritos, milk cartons, and soda cans.

Nicole whipped a pile of books off the seat beside her, and Stacey dropped into the chair gratefully.

"What took you so long?" Nicole asked.

"Irregular verbs," Stacey explained. "Tiny Hurst asked a question just as the bell rang, and Madame Stemmer made us all sit there and listen to the answer. 'You go when I say go, not when a bell rings.' You know the routine."

"So she talks me into this *major overhaul*." Lee Whitaker's voice rose and every face at the table turned toward her. "It cost a fortune and took forever, but she was right. At least, that's what I *thought*. My hair looked great. Perfect. I was thrilled. And I go to my cousin's house—in St. Louis, you know?—and I jump into his pool—and my whole head turns absolutely *green!*"

Laughter rippled up one side of the table and down the other. Glancing sideways at Nicole, who was soaking in Lee's every word, Stacey could read the expression on her face as clearly as the morning's computer screen: If Nicole could have dyed her hair green right then and there, she would have done it.

A few short months ago, Stacey would have felt the exact same way. She and Nicole would have laughed about it: Oh, to have Lee's incredible *style!* Ah, well, mediocrity loves company. At least we have each other.

Did they still? Sitting right beside her at the table, Nicole seemed miles and miles away.

"I mean, there I am in St. Louis," Lee went on, "with all these really terrific guys my cousin knows, and *green hair.*"

"What did you do?" Tanya Breuer asked. She'd completely forgotten the sandwich in her hand, left it poised in midair, and Robbie Dougherty was sliding a slice of roast beef right out of it.

"My aunt took me to her hairdresser," Lee said, laughing as Tanya slapped Robbie's hand and reclaimed her sandwich. "He cut off as much as he could and treated the rest with this neutralizer stuff."

"You can't tell a thing," Cassie Daniels said.

"It's all grown in now. But believe me, it was green. Not slightly green. Oh, no! Kermit the Frog green. I can never go back to St. Louis."

"Oh, sure you can," Cassie told her.

Lee giggled. "Well, actually, I can," she admitted, twisting the stem off the apple on her tray. "I'm invited to the Octoberfest at the Academy. There was this cadet—of course, I didn't know he was a cadet when I met him. He was in a bathing suit—"

Lee's story went on, with a few more jokes about the green hair and through a week of dates with the cadet.

"He's written me almost every day since I got back," she concluded.

Girls sighed and boys nudged each other and hooted. Lee winked at no one in particular and took a dainty bite of her apple.

"Any cadets in the Berkshires?" Nicole asked, scooting a burnt Tator Tot off her tray.

Stacey shook her head. "Actors."

"Oh, yeah? Anybody famous?"

"Not yet. But they will be. They were good. And they really taught me a lot."

"You mean you actually talked to them?"

"I auditioned. That's what I've been trying to tell you, Nicole. My brother said to try it. They were doing *The Music Man*, and they needed townspeople for the big parade. So I went. And I got in."

"No kidding!"

"No kidding." At last, Stacey had Nicole's full attention. Now she could share her story before she burst! "After *Music Man*, I volunteered to help backstage for the rest of the summer. I built sets and ran props and helped the actors study their lines.

"That's when my folks freaked out. I mean, it was cute when I was just pretending to play one of seventy-six trombones, but when I started getting really involved, they couldn't handle it. Their innocent baby hanging out with wild and wacky theater people! My mom fretted, and my dad wanted to pack up and come home. If it wasn't for my brother and sister-in-law smoothing things over—and the grandbaby learning how to play peekaboo—I'd've been back here ordering burgers from you weeks ago."

"Wild and wacky, huh?" Nicole drawled, a mischievous sparkle lighting her hazel eyes. "Sounds like great fun!"

Stacey shifted in her chair impatiently. Nicole was not getting the point at all. "It was more than fun, Nicole," she tried to explain. "I've never met people like that before. They were so passionate about what they were doing. They talked theater morning, noon, and . . ."

"Passionate," Nicole echoed, making the word sound as silly as Caroline's nail polish. Suddenly, Nicole spun away. "Lee! You'll never guess who walked into Burger Chef last weekend. On my next-to-last day!"

Lee turned her bright blue gaze on Nicole, and everyone at the table listened up. "Who?"

"Barry Darrow. You remember him? The senior we used to follow around the neighborhood when we were in sixth grade?"

Lee put down her apple. "Barry Darrow?"

"I swear."

"Did he remember you?"

"Not at first. But I reminded him. Then he did. I think. He's in medical school."

"I always wondered what happened to him," Lee said.

Nicole giggled. "Me, too. And he's cuter than ever. I think I'm going to become a doctor."

"Or a patient," Lee suggested. "It's worth a try!"

Stacey stuffed the last of her ham sandwich back into its plastic bag and stood up. "I'm—uh—I left something in my locker," she said.

No one at the table noticed, not even Nicole.

Stacey fled to the girls' room and closed herself into a stall. Tears spilled from her eyes. She fumbled in her purse for a tissue and angrily wiped the tears away. Why wouldn't Nicole *listen?* Wasn't it bad enough Stacey's parents didn't understand or care about this new world that meant so much to her? She'd counted on Nicole's support. Wasn't that what best friends were for?

13

Two of a kind. Maybe they had been, before, trailing in Lee's shadow, at the edge of the in crowd. But no more.

Once Stacey would have told Nicole every detail of an experience, watching carefully to see if it met with her approval. But what kinds of experiences had they been? A night of baby-sitting? A phone conversation with a boy? The search for a new pair of jeans? A nod from Nicole meant a nod from the whole group. It meant Stacey was still within the bounds of normalcy, of official in-crowd Oakview High School behavior. She would not be tossed out to make her way among the losers, hunched over her books, eyes on the ground, forever walking, sitting, eating, breathing beyond the fringes of acceptability.

Suddenly Stacey found herself crying even harder. She pressed both fists to her mouth, afraid someone would hear. She and Nicole had been foolish, sure. But they'd played the only game they knew. And they'd played it *together*. Now that was over. She couldn't take Nicole with her where she was going, couldn't even make her understand how far she'd already gone. How she wished she could! But it wasn't possible. That wasn't Nicole's fault, or her own. It was just the way things had worked out.

The summer was hers alone. It had not touched anyone else at Oakview, and it never would. It had happened only to her, and it had changed her. If she wanted to keep it whole—and she did, she *had* to—she would have to keep it to herself.

She sucked in a long, trembling breath and left the stall. As she stopped to dab at her eyes again in front of a mirror, the bell rang, signaling the end of first lunch hour. Outside the girls' room, the hall buzzed as she hurried toward English lit.

English lit! All right! At last, a ray of hope. She had Mr. Barclay again, and he was her absolutely favorite teacher.

He would have loved the people at Lakeside Playhouse. They could quote Shakespeare for hours. They knew Eugene O'Neill and Arthur Miller and Tennessee Williams and dozens of names Stacey had never even heard of. They spoke of them with awe, drawing lines from the plays lovingly from their mouths, arguing the meaning beyond the words, remembering the best actors they'd seen in each role, dreaming of the roles they'd one day play.

Were there any cadets up there? Nicole had asked. Stacey almost laughed aloud. What would Nicole make of Randy Elliot, his long, bony nose poking out from under the wide-brimmed brown felt hat he wore offstage every minute of the day, his jeans and plaid shirt ratty and faded with washings, his bare feet gnarled and callused? Creep, she'd probably say. Geek. Nerd. But what would she think when he took the stage at night in *Our Town*, transformed into the young husband, George, aching with grief for his lost Emily?

Carole Dumont's fair-skinned, delicate face rose up in front of Stacey. If Randy was a lot cooler than he looked, Carole was a lot tougher. Like the others, she performed one role at night, rehearsed another in the morning, and polished yet a third in the afternoon to keep up with the constantly changing repertory.

Stacey had helped her study her lines. One time, Stacey had glanced up after reading George's part and found Carole looking straight at her as she recited Emily's response. But it wasn't Carole's face she saw—not even the eyes were Carole's. They were Emily's. And the words came not from a script, but from Emily's heart, as if she were truly saying them for the first time. Stacey had been so taken aback by the transformation, she'd forgotten to read the next line. The face, the smile, the eyes that waited for her to go on were Emily's.

How did actors *do* that? Stacey's pace quickened. Bodies flew past her. People waved or called out "Hi!" but she barely noticed them. She had so much to learn. She'd do it, though. She'd already begun to read plays and books on acting technique and biographies of great playwrights and actors. She would study until she could change her face and body and voice and become a thousand people, alive in a thousand lives.

Nothing could stop her, not her parents' objections, not Nicole's indifference, not even a flood of Passion de Nuit. Next summer she would be an apprentice. After that, she would study theater in college. And she would become one of them—the people in love with the work they did and the enchantment they created, with making plays, worlds more real than the real one, their colors brighter, their sounds richer, their feelings truer.

She slid into a seat in the front row of Mr. Barclay's class and checked the room, by habit, for familiar faces: Tanya, Walt, Dawn Covington, Cassie Daniels. Stacey returned their smiles and waves.

Still, she was alone. Okay. Use everything, the actors had told her. Store it; save it. Nothing is wasted; no one is insignificant. An actor feeds on life. Stacey vowed to use this senior year, right down to the last minute, loneliness included. Fall, winter, spring.

And then the doors will open, she promised herself, and I will be *out of here.*

LEFTOVERS

"Leftovers inside," the note said. "Back late. XX, Mother and Dad."

Cassie Daniels opened the refrigerator door and poked at the plastic bowls on the top shelf. Tuna salad. A couple of tomato slices on a bed of lettuce already wilting around the edges. Two English muffins in their plastic wrapper and a lump of cheddar cheese. She sighed and let the door swing shut.

This was the third leftover night of the week. *And* it was Friday. People should *not* be alone on Friday nights with wilting lettuce and lumps of cheese, Cassie told herself. While her parents were out chasing fame and fortune, she could at least have pizza with a friend.

She lifted off the lid of a ceramic cookie jar in the shape of a Siamese cat and dumped the family mad money onto the counter. Twenty-seven dollars and sixty-three cents. All right! That was one good thing about her parents: They also provided leftover cash.

A glance at the clock above the stove told Cassie it was early, not even five-thirty. She picked up the phone and dialed Lee Whitaker's private number. Lee's hello interrupted the third ring.

"Lee? It's Cassie. Want to go out for pizza?"

There was a pause.

"Lee? You there?"

"Yeah, yeah, I'm here, Cass. You—ah—caught me at a bad time. I'm a—a little short of money."

"Hey, no problem," Cassie assured her. "My treat."

"Well, thanks, Cass, that's really very sweet, but, see, I'm baby-sitting tonight. As a matter of fact, I was just on my way out. I'm supposed to give the kids dinner."

17

"I could bring the pizza over," Cassie offered. "Where will you be?"

"Oh, no, no. I don't think these people would like that," Lee broke in. "They're pretty strict about guests and all. You know how it is."

"Oh, sure," Cassie said, suddenly feeling very small in the emptiness of her house. "How late do you have to sit? Maybe we could do something after."

"Um—I'm not sure," Lee replied. "They didn't say."

"Give me their number," Cassie said. "I'll call you."

"No, listen, Cass, I'll call you, okay? If they're getting back early enough. I'll ask them as soon as I get there, okay? If you don't hear from me in half an hour or so, you'll know they're staying out late and I'm stuck."

"Half an hour." Cassie checked the stove clock. "Like about six?"

"Right," Lee agreed. "No later than six. But if I don't call, you'll know I'm tied up till late."

"Not really tied up, I hope," Cassie said.

Lee chuckled. "Right. Not really. Listen, I've got to go, Cass. Talk to you later. Bye."

Cassie hung up the phone, still smiling. Chatting with Lee could do that for her. Everybody was crazy about Lee. They couldn't even be jealous about her winning everything all the time—cheerleading captain, homecoming queen. She deserved it. Lee was what Cassie's mother called top of the line.

Cassie decided to get in a quick shower before Lee called back. In no time, she was in and out and padding down the hall to her parents' bedroom, light brown ringlets poking out of one plush white towel, bony elbows pressing another towel to her body. The red light on the answering machine on her dad's night table stared up at her, unblinking. Good. She hadn't missed Lee's call. It was only a quarter to six anyway. Plenty of time.

Back in her own room, Cassie pulled on a new baby blue sweatsuit and began the ordeal of blow-drying her hair, yanking at it with a brush to pull the kinks out. "Oh, Cassie, I wish my hair was curly like yours," she squealed at her reflection in the mirror. It was always some stunning blonde with a perfect blunt cut brushing her shoulders who said it. What in the world were they all wishing for—curls that undid the most expensive haircuts on earth, that outwitted blow-dryers, jumbo curlers, spray, mousse, glop, gunk—you name it—to scrunch themselves up any old way they wanted to, like the frizz on a clown's head? Is that what they all wanted? Fine. Here. Take it.

Cassie dropped the still-roaring dryer onto her dressing table and grabbed two fistfuls of hair, pretending to rip them out by the roots. Well, not exactly pretending. She would if she could—

The phone.

She fumbled the dryer into silence and took the path to her parents' bedside in a half dozen giant steps. "Lee?" she gasped into the phone.

"What?" a male voice asked. "Who is this?"

"Who is *this*?"

"I must have the wrong number," the voice mumbled.

"No! Wait!" Cassie begged. If this was an important call for her parents and she messed up, she was dead. "Who are you calling? I mean, whom? Please."

"What?"

"What?"

"Cassie? Is this Cassie Daniels?"

"Yes, yes, this is Cassie Daniels! Who are *you*?"

"Tiny Hurst."

"Tiny Hurst?" It couldn't be. Why on earth—?

"Keith," the voice went on. "Tiny's my nickname. Kind of. I mean, it's what everybody at school calls me. I sit behind you in French 2."

Cassie pictured the lug who breathed down her neck all through French, taller even than the basketball players, but gawky and slow-moving.

"I know where you sit, Tiny," she said coolly. "What is it you want?"

"I thought maybe you'd like to go out for pizza or something tonight."

How did he know? Did Lee—? No, he couldn't have spoken to Lee. Lee was practically out the door when Cassie called her.

"How did you get my number?"

"I looked it up in the phone book," Tiny explained. "Actually, I was kind of surprised you didn't have an unlisted number. I mean, everybody sees your dad on the news. I figured there'd be nuts calling him all the time. But there it was—Jason Daniels. It didn't say 'anchorman,' though. I thought maybe it would, you know, like sometimes it says 'attorney-at-law' next to a name. But it didn't."

Cassie closed her eyes and sank onto the bed. I can't believe this, she thought, as Tiny's voice droned on in her ear. When she opened her eyes, her dad's digital clock read 6:24. For a moment, panic chilled her heart, and she sat bolt upright. Had Lee tried to call? No, they had call waiting. She fell back against the pillow.

The buzz in her ear got louder. Tiny was getting back around to the pizza. Oh, what the heck, Cassie thought. Lee was obviously stuck with those kids for the night. Might as well give the guy a thrill. Besides, she was hungry, and not for leftover tuna.

20

"Pick me up in half an hour," she said, breaking into Tiny's monologue.

"Okay! See you then!"

"Okay," Cassie echoed, without his enthusiasm. "See you."

Thirty-eight minutes later, she knew she'd made a dreadful mistake. She was in Tiny Hurst's car—a rusting Ford station wagon that smelled a little like—tuna?—and they were chugging down Southern Hills Avenue toward Angelino's Pizzeria at the mall.

Everyone there would know her, including Angelino. He did his own commercials on her dad's evening news: "Mama, she's with the angels now, but her recipe's in Eli, with her boy, Angelino." Cassie's mother had helped produce that piece of fluff and a lot of other local commercials that were even worse. Aluminum siding. Pig feed. How could her mother live with herself? "Pigs have to eat, too," she'd explained, shrugging off Cassie's complaints. But Cassie knew her mother was dying to get out of Eli to a bigger TV station with top-of-the-line clients.

Well, that was her problem. Cassie had her own to worry about. Everyone at Angelino's who knew Cassie would also know she was out on a Friday night with Tiny Hurst. What would they make of it? Tiny was definitely not top of the line. He probably wasn't even *in* line. Come to think of it, Lee Whitaker made a point of avoiding him.

"You know what I really feel like?" Cassie said, on a sudden inspiration. "Smokey's Barbeque. Yeah. I haven't had barbeque in ages. Come to think of it, I just had pizza yesterday. Pull in over there, Tiny. No, *there*. You can turn around in that parking lot."

The Ford lunged into a fast left turn. Two tires jumped the curb as Tiny wheeled in and out of the lot. "Smokey's it is," he said cheerfully, and headed north again.

Cassie breathed a sigh of relief. Smokey advertised on Channel 10, too, but nobody important ever went there. He did make a mean combo platter, though. Cassie tightened her stomach muscles to muffle the empty rumbling.

Just north of the public square, Smokey's was one of the few downtown businesses that had survived the building of the mall on Eli's south side. "It's as if this town had a heart transplant," Cassie's dad observed when they'd moved here a year ago. "Downtown's practically dead, and the south side looks like a sprawl searching for its lost soul." "It's a growing market" was all Cassie's mother made of it.

Tiny had no trouble finding a parking spot right in front of the restaurant. Forcing his door open with one huge shoulder, he bounded around the front of the wagon to help Cassie battle the rust and dents holding her side shut. The tattered Halloween skeleton barely visible in Smokey's dim front window struck Cassie as oddly appropriate. If anyone saw her crawling out of this pathetic excuse for a car, she was dead.

A bell tinkled as they entered the restaurant. Cassie had been here for lunch with her parents, but the narrow room looked even more dingy after dark. A long counter ran down one side, facing a dozen mismatched wooden tables, all of them unoccupied, thank goodness. The floor was worn and bare; paper pumpkins, witches, ghosts, and cats dangled listlessly from the walls. Behind the counter, a tall, gaunt girl about Cassie's age picked at a hangnail on one of her thumbs and watched them come in without a great show of interest.

"Hi," Tiny greeted her. "I know you from somewhere, don't I?"

The girl shrugged and dropped her eyes to the counter,

where she found and snatched up her order pad and a pencil. "Can I help you?" she asked in a hoarse voice.

Tiny slid onto one of the counter stools. "You go to Oakview, right?"

The girl nodded. She seemed puzzled by his attention. Cassie tugged at Tiny's shirt sleeve and tilted her head toward one of the tables.

"Wait a minute," he said and turned back to the waitress. "World geography? Mr. Sanchez?"

The girl's head bobbed again.

"Got it!" Tiny cried triumphantly. "I'm Tiny Hurst. Keith. But you can call me Tiny. What's your name?"

"Tara," the girl barely whispered. She kept her eyes lowered and a death grip on the pad and pencil.

"Tara. That's nice. Guess your mom liked *Gone with the Wind* a lot, huh? Well, hi, Tara. Nice to meet you."

Cassie yanked a menu out of its metal holder and shoved it into Tiny's hands. "Shall we order something?" she asked impatiently.

"I knew I knew her," Tiny insisted.

"Big deal," Cassie snapped. "I'll have the combo platter."

"Okay," Tara said flatly and edged back toward a doorway at the far end of the counter.

"Me, too," Tiny told her. "Only I'd like a jumbo sandwich instead of the regular and a double order of fries."

Tara scribbled on her pad and disappeared into the kitchen.

Cassie dropped into a chair. "Is somebody joining us?" she asked, as Tiny finally left the counter and lumbered over.

"I'm hungry," he said, scraping his chair against the floor as he pulled it closer. "I'm always hungry. I'm big and I have a very high metabolism. It runs in my family.

23

Which is lucky—the metabolism—because otherwise we'd all weigh a ton. We like to eat even when we're not hungry. Last weekend . . ."

He stopped short and threw Cassie an amused glance.

"And when we're nervous, we talk too much," he finished lamely. "You want to go to a movie after we eat?"

How do I get out of this? Cassie wondered. She wanted to go home. No, she wanted to *be* home, *right now.* Like in the movies. Blackout. Instant change of scene. Cassie at home.

Alone.

Oh, well, a movie was a movie. It would pass the time, and it would be dark. At least she and Tiny would have something to talk about—which movie to see—while they stuffed their faces. Cassie wondered which movie would be the least likely to attract anybody from Oakview.

"Okay," she heard herself say.

They decided on the Tom Cruise at Cinema 6 in the old shopping center on the north side of town, not far from Smokey's. No one from Oakview would go there, not even for Tom Cruise. Cassie was sure of that.

But she was wrong. Jamie Bingham and Sam Weinstadt were in the theater lobby. Cassie spotted them through the plate glass window as she and Tiny crossed the parking lot. Thank goodness she'd seen them first!

"Listen, Tiny, I've really got to go to the ladies' room," she said. "You go on and get the tickets and I'll meet you inside, okay? Tell you what. Just take a seat in the back row and I'll find you."

"How will you get in without a ticket?" Tiny asked.

"Show them you've bought two. They'll let me in."

It worked, smooth as cream. A fast "hi" to the guys and into the ladies' room before they could even ask who she was with. Whom. Then ten minutes of arguing with her hair. The theater was already dark when she located Tiny in the back row, loaded down with giant Cokes and a tub of buttered popcorn.

The movie wasn't half bad; the Coke was an excuse to make a beeline back to the ladies' room before the lights came up; and by the time the two of them hit the parking lot again, practically everybody else was gone. A perfect evening, considering.

Tiny was quiet all the way home. Fine with me, Cassie told herself. She managed to get the wagon door jerked open the second he pulled into the drive. "Thanks for everything," she said brightly, one foot already on the blacktop. "I had a great time."

"I'm not stupid, you know," Tiny replied, staring straight ahead at the windshield.

Cassie felt her face go red. She ducked back into the car and pulled her foot in after her. "I never said you were."

"I didn't get it at first—Smokey's instead of Angelino's. But when you took up residence in the ladies' room, I finally caught on."

"I beg your pardon?"

"When I called you earlier," he said, "you thought it was going to be Lee Whitaker, didn't you?"

"Maybe I did. So what?" Cassie answered. "She's my best friend."

Tiny snorted and turned around to face her. "You're even slower than I am! She's not your best friend. She's not anybody's best friend—except her own."

"Don't you talk about Lee that way," Cassie warned him. "She is too my best friend. We do stuff together all the time."

"You mean *she* does stuff and you tag around after her. I see you at school. You look like a lost puppy."

"We do stuff after school, too," Cassie insisted. "I went

to the mall with her just last week. And who are you calling a dog?"

"I said puppy," Tiny replied. "It's a figure of speech. Look, I don't understand what's going on here. If you didn't want to go out with me, why didn't you just say so?"

Cassie was at a loss for words. How could she tell a guy he just wasn't . . . top of the line? And why *had* she gone out with him? Was one Friday evening alone that unbearable? It wouldn't have been the first. . . .

"I guess you've decided I'm a creep," Tiny said, as if he'd been reading her mind. "But that doesn't make me one. At least I know where I stand. Lee hangs out with you when there's nobody else around to play with. Same as you went out with me tonight."

"I went out with you tonight because I felt sorry for you," Cassie snapped, fighting back tears. She was *not* going to let Tiny Hurst see her cry! And what was she crying about anyway? What she needed to do right then and there was to make him see just how insignificant he really was. "I happen to know Lee Whitaker doesn't think a whole lot of you," she went on, "which means you don't have a friend in our whole school worth having. It figures, if losers like that Tara person are the best you can dig up. So I was being nice to you, okay? And look at the thanks I get."

Instead of matching her anger, Tiny threw back his big head and guffawed. "I appreciate your concern," he said, "but I have all the friends I need, thank you very much."

"In that case, why did you bother to ask me out?"

Tiny gave her a slow grin. He wasn't the worst-looking guy in the world, but something about him made her absolutely furious. The more uncomfortable she felt, the calmer he seemed to get. Now he leaned against his door, one arm resting along the seat back between them. His fingertips almost touched her shoulder. She wriggled out of reach.

"I like the way you speak French," he said. "And I thought you were different. I knew you weren't really Lee's type."

"Well, I am most certainly not *your* type!" Cassie gasped. She climbed out of the wagon, banging her knee as she struggled to slam its creaky door behind her. Trying hard not to limp, she reached the path on Tiny's side of the car. "I would have been out with Lee tonight," she informed him, "but she had to baby-sit."

Tiny rolled down his window. "Is that what she told you?" he asked. "Funny thing—she was at that movie we just saw."

"She was not!"

"Was too. She probably drove all the way up there just to avoid you. Wouldn't that be ironic?"

"Liar!" Cassie screamed. But even as the shrill sound hung for an instant in the crisp October air, she knew he could be telling the truth.

Why? Why would Lee do that to her?

She almost felt grateful when Tiny got out of the car and leaned against its pockmarked hood. He filled up some of the vast, empty space surrounding her.

"She was at the movie," he said quietly. "I saw her come in, and I saw her leave. While you were in the ladies' room, I had plenty of time to look around."

"She brought little kids to see that movie?" Cassie asked, already knowing the answer.

"She wasn't there with little kids," Tiny said. "She was with a couple of guys from school."

Cassie opened her mouth to protest. Then she closed it. Jamie and Sam had been waiting there in the lobby for

Lee. Lee had gone to the movies with both of them and not invited her. But why?

"I'm sorry," Tiny said softly.

Cassie nodded. All of a sudden, she just felt tired. "Thanks," she said, moving toward her house. "For dinner and all. I had—"

Tiny waved her off. "It's okay," he said. "See you Monday in French 2. I sit behind you."

Cassie almost managed a grin. "I know," she said.

He waited until she was safely inside before driving off. From the living room window, she watched the station wagon's taillights disappear into the night. Okay, she thought, so he isn't a creep. But what *is* he?

Tiny Hurst was one of those people who managed to get by without a label. Cassie didn't have time for people like that. She'd been to four schools since fifth grade, following her parents' journey toward TV stardom, and she'd always managed to find the in crowd and join them. People like Tiny made life too complicated. It was like lobbing tennis balls at somebody who wouldn't raise his racquet to hit them back. They knew the rules but didn't even try to play by them. No wonder he got on her nerves! Lee was smart to write him off.

At ten o'clock the next morning, the phone rang, and it was Lee.

"Hey, Cass! Want to go to the mall?" she asked, cheerful as ever.

Cassie slogged a spoon around in her Wheat Chex. "Anybody else going?" she asked.

"No," Lee said. "I called around. Nobody's home."

Cassie struggled to pull in a deep breath. "How'd the baby-sitting go?" she asked.

"It didn't," Lee chirped. "I got all the way over there and they hung around and hung around and then they canceled; can you believe that? One of the kids was throwing up. I tried to call you, but you were gone. So I went to a movie."

"There was no message on the machine," Cassie said cautiously, then held her breath.

"Oh, I hung up," Lee explained. "I hate those things. I never know what to say."

The air rushed from Cassie's lungs, leaving her feeling giddy. Tiny was wrong, wrong about Lee, wrong about their friendship. "Me, too," she said. "But my parents insist. Any minute now, CBS might be calling them up to bigger and better things."

"Do they do that?" Lee asked. "CBS? Just call people like your mom and dad out of the blue?"

"I guess so," Cassie said. "You know Mother and Dad—they live on dreams and important dinners with all the right people. I live on leftovers."

"You never got your pizza?" Lee asked.

"Oh, well, no. I changed my mind," Cassie said.

"So where'd you go?"

"Oh—out."

"Anything special?"

"Nah—just—oh, you know, out. Nothing great."

"I know what you mean," Lee said sympathetically. "So—how about the mall?"

"Well, *sure*," Cassie sang into the phone.

It was obvious Lee hadn't spotted her at the movie with Tiny. But what if Tiny told other people at school? What if he started hanging around her, as if they were—friends? She had nearly two semesters of high school left. She couldn't spend all that time hiding in ladies' rooms!

"There are people who can get you where you want to go," her mother always said, "and others who just get in your way. Choose wisely."

29

Cassie would have to cut Tiny dead. Set him straight, fast. He liked to know where he stood; fine, she'd be the first to tell him.

A chilly rain fell as she hurried into school Monday morning. There was Lee, in the middle of the usual crowd. Above her head, a filmy ghost in a football helmet floated across a bulletin board. "Touchdown!" it proclaimed. "Join the Oakview Booo-oo-oo-sters!"

"Hi, Lee!" Cassie called.

"Hi, Cass!" Lee took time for a quick smile while half a dozen other voices clamored for her attention.

The group had already begun moving down the hall when Cassie finished stuffing her raincoat and books inside her locker. She trotted behind, just making the tail end when the first-hour warning bell sounded. "See you at lunch, Lee," she called. Lee's hand fluttered briefly in her direction.

Cassie fidgeted through her first two classes, then braced herself and headed for Madame Stemmer's room. There he was, so big he made the desk look as if it belonged to a kindergartner. Heart pounding, Cassie bent her head and fussed with her books as she crossed the room.

"Hi, Cassie," he said.

"Hi." A quick smile, And that was it, she told herself, slipping into her seat. Do not turn around, not now, not ever. He's got to understand.

Apparently, he did. The class, pop quiz and all, whizzed by without another peep out of him. He sprang from his seat and was gone the minute the bell rang. They had the same lunch hour, but Cassie was so busy jockeying for a seat near Lee, she hardly had time to notice him, two tables down, sitting with Walt Hightower and Ian Mac-Laine. *Ian MacLaine,* whose house was a neighborhood

30

eyesore! His father was supposedly a lawyer, but he kept the property looking like a dump.

So that was what Tiny called having all the friends he needed! Pathetic.

Everyone at Cassie's table was laughing at something Lee said. Cassie wasn't sure what the joke was but joined in anyway, then opened her container of milk with a happy sigh. She was home safe. She'd made a mistake going out with Tiny—well, she'd done it out of kindness. And now it was over. Amen.

She almost didn't bother to read the note on the refrigerator door when she got home that afternoon, but a row of exclamation points caught her eye. "Looks like Indianapolis next!!!!!!!!!!" it said. "Maybe January or February. Keep your fingers crossed! XX, Mother and Dad. P.S. Leftovers inside."

Cassie opened the refrigerator. The same plastic bowls stood in their neat little row. She slammed the door shut without removing anything. Oh, who cares? she thought, a lump rising in her throat. She wasn't hungry anyway.

BOYS ARE EASY

"Boys," Lee Whitaker announced, settling back against her fluffed-up pillow, "are like puppies. Show them a little kindness and they'll follow you anywhere."

Nicole Drake sat cross-legged at the foot of the queen-sized bed, facing Lee. "Follow you, maybe," she said, plucking at a loose thread in the rose-covered quilt. "But there's nobody following me—and I'm not exactly the Wicked Witch of the West."

"Not the same thing," Lee said. "Not being cruel is not the same thing as showing a little kindness. Showing a little kindness isn't even the same thing as being kind. Actually, you can even *be* the Wicked Witch of the West, and they'll *still* follow you, once they're hooked. Everybody knows you can kick a dog and it'll lick your hand."

Lee wriggled onto her side and sifted through a stack of cassette tapes on her night table. Nicole sighed as she watched Lee's perfectly cut blonde hair cascade forward across her unblemished cheek.

Lee looked pretty—and *right*—no matter what she did. She could dribble ketchup down the front of a brand-new sweater at a party and not be embarrassed by it. In fact, she'd make every other girl in the room wish she could drip something down the front of *her* best outfit, too. Only, if someone else tried it, she'd end up alone in the kitchen, soaking the front of her clothes with water from the tap, while Lee *still* would have a circle of guys around her in the living room.

There were three ways, as far as Nicole could see, to be popular with boys. Having reached her senior year at Oakview without one serious boyfriend, she'd decided to make a last-ditch, comprehensive study of the subject. The easiest way to be popular, she'd observed, was to already have a boyfriend. When guys knew you were spoken for, they relaxed and talked to you and joked around and even flirted with you.

The second way was to be wild. There were always guys willing to join you in that. Of course, they were usually the same guys you'd cross the street to avoid, like Dub Colby and the other animals in Last Chance Language Arts. But if you were crazy enough to want them, they were available.

Nicole had no boyfriend, not even the prospect of one, and she was not wild. That left only one other choice: to be like Lee. Lee could have any guy she wanted. All she had to do was decide on one, and the next thing you knew, he was on the phone, asking her out.

It didn't matter if she had another boyfriend at the time or not. And she certainly wasn't wild. She didn't drink or smoke or anything. In fact, Nicole had once heard Tiny Hurst refer to Lee as the Ice Queen. Whatever Lee had, she kept it to herself, but boys lined up all the same.

"I don't get it," Nicole said. "I don't understand how you do it. Has there ever been a guy you wanted that you didn't get?"

"Nope," Lee admitted. She inserted a cassette and listened for a moment as a drumbeat pulsed through the giant speakers across the room. When the melody began, she turned the volume down and repositioned herself against the pillow. "Toss the puppy a bone," she said, as if that explained everything.

Nicole shuddered. "They don't look like puppies to me," she said.

"That's your problem," Lee informed her. "You let them scare you."

"They're bigger than I am," Nicole pointed out. "And

stronger. And they hold all the cards. I mean, you can ask one out now and then, like if it's a Ladies Pay All dance, but if you do it too often, you're desperate. Nine times out of ten, they get to choose—or not choose. I can't stand being looked at that way—like clothes on a fifty-percent-off rack."

"And it shows in your face," Lee said. "And that's why you don't get chosen."

"I sometimes get chosen," Nicole protested, even though she knew exactly what Lee meant and that she was right.

"Not as often as you'd like," Lee said. "Which should be *whenever* you like. It should be up to you, not them. It's not 'Oh, choose me, oh, please, choose me.' It's 'Pray real hard, buster, and maybe I'll let you get lucky.' You're the master; he's the puppy."

Nicole giggled. "I'm afraid of dogs, too."

"Puppies?"

"Well, no, I guess not puppies."

"There you go, then. Think puppies."

Lee swung her legs off the bed and padded barefooted across the thick rose-colored carpet to her closet. "Okay," she went on, "you want a date. Craig Howard and my cousin Ray are coming in from St. Louis for Thanksgiving. I'll fix you up with Ray. You'd be cute together."

Panic shot through Nicole's heart. A blind date? With Lee's cousin?

Craig Howard was Lee's cadet, the guy she'd met at her cousin's house in St. Louis and had been raving about ever since. He and Ray were in some posh academy together. They were definitely not puppies.

And blind dates were the worst. Nicole had been through that scene once too often. It meant sitting in the backseat of somebody's car, pretending not to notice that the couple in the front seat were in danger of permanently welding their lips together, while her own date cleared his throat a lot and made awkward grabs and lunges at parts of her face and body because he thought he had to. Whatever they did or didn't do, she and her date ended up miserable, feeling more like strangers than ever. Eventually he'd retreat in embarrassment and they would sit there, silhouetted against the steamed-up windows, waiting for the front seat to cool down and wishing for a quick and merciful death.

Lee was getting bored with her; Nicole could tell. It was a rare enough day when she had Lee all to herself, and now she'd blown it with her boy problems. But she couldn't date Lee's cousin. If it didn't work out, he wouldn't disappear like the others. He'd be Lee's cousin forever, remembering the time he took out her friend Nicole, the loser. She'd be what they reminisced and laughed about at family gatherings—the official Whitaker Thanksgiving turkey.

"Let's go for a walk," Lee said. "It's getting stuffy in here."

"What I want," Nicole told her, catching the Oakview sweatshirt Lee pitched at her from the depths of her walk-in closet, "is not a blind date. I want to learn how to toss the puppy a bone."

Lee pulled on a Washington University sweatshirt, another souvenir of her St. Louis conquests. "You want to learn how to flirt, you mean?"

"Yes," Nicole said.

Lee cocked her head toward the bedroom door. Nicole obediently yanked on the borrowed sweatshirt and followed her downstairs and outside. It was a glorious November afternoon. The huge maples lining Lee's wide street were brilliant with their last show of color, and there was a crisp layer of leaves on the sidewalk, just right for crunching and kicking. Lee headed toward the small artificial lake at the center of the subdivision.

"All right," she said, "there are a couple of ways we can do this. I can tell you what to do, and you can just do it. Or you can watch me in action—and sort of take notes. And then do it."

"Or we could do both at once," Nicole suggested. "You could tell me what you're going to do; I could watch you do it; and then I could try it myself, step by step."

"Perfect," Lee agreed. "Maximum impact."

At the top of the hill above the lake, Nicole paused and took a deep breath. The air held just a hint of winter coolness under the warmth of the slanting afternoon sun. It was invigorating. Everything seemed possible. "When do we start?" she asked, bouncing down the hill to catch up with Lee.

"Whenever you want," Lee said. "But that's not the first question, is it? Don't we have to decide who we're starting *with?*"

"That's easy. Brian Marsh," Nicole replied.

"Brian Marsh," Lee repeated thoughtfully, then nodded. "Piece of cake. He's not even going with anyone."

"Well, of course not," Nicole said. "If he were, I wouldn't have picked him."

"Why not?" Lee asked. "All's fair in love and war."

"You mean you'd make a play for somebody else's boyfriend?"

"If a girl can't hang on to her own boyfriend," Lee argued, "she doesn't have much of a grip on him to begin with, does she?"

Nicole sucked in another deep breath and let it whistle out between her lips as she thought over this new angle. "I don't need the competition," she finally decided. "I can't even attract a guy like Brian, who's running around loose."

"Have you tried?"

"Well, I say hello whenever I see him. He says hello back, most of the time. But I'm not even sure he knows who I am."

"Do you smile when you say hello?"

"I don't know. Probably not. I get too nervous."

"You have to smile. And it wouldn't hurt to wink."

"Wink?" Nicole gasped. "You actually wink at them?"

"Sure. It makes them feel like there's already something going on between us."

"What if they don't *want* to think that?"

"But they do. Guys are very insecure, Nicole. It's true, they get to do the choosing, but they want to know ahead of time that you'll choose them back. Every guy feels like a jerk until some girl tells him otherwise. A wink says right off the bat you think he's special. It's an act of kindness."

"A bone for the puppy."

"Exactly. And that's the way you have to think of it, too, that you're doing him a big favor. Because you are. And because otherwise you come across looking desperate."

Nicole rolled her eyes. Chances were good on that.

Lee sat on the grass a few yards above the edge of the lake. Two pairs of swans, one black and the other white, glided over the surface of the water. Across the way, mallard ducks argued noisily under the bare branches of a weeping willow.

Nicole flopped down beside Lee. The ground was surprisingly cold beneath her jeans.

Lee closed her eyes and tilted her face toward the sun. "So—who do you want me to work on for your demonstration? Pick a boy, any boy."

"Don't you want to pick your own?" Nicole asked.

"No," Lee said. "I'm at my best when I'm not too involved."

Amazed, but quickly deciding Lee was the expert after all, Nicole ran through the guys in their crowd. The best were all spoken for. She searched the edges for acceptable fringe types, like Brian Marsh—guys who weren't at the center of things but who weren't considered hopelessly out of it, either.

"Jamie Bingham?"

"Sexy," Lee mused out loud. "But totally in love with his guitar. How much time do you want to spend on this project?"

"I was hoping for immediate results."

"Then skip Jamie."

"Okay. How about Walt Hightower?"

Lee interrupted her sun worshiping to toss Nicole an astonished glance. "Are you serious? He's a baby."

Nicole scrunched up one shoulder apologetically. "He only skipped one grade. And he's awfully cute."

"He's a buddy, Nicole, not a boyfriend. I do not date sixteen-year-olds."

Nicole sighed. "Tiny Hurst?" she suggested.

Lee shook her head.

"Why not?"

"Not my type."

"He's cute, too," Nicole pointed out, "in a teddy bear way. A large teddy bear."

Or a very large puppy, it suddenly occurred to her. Funny, she'd never thought about it before, but Tiny was one boy who never made her nervous. Of course, they'd practically grown up in each other's houses. He lived right down the street, and their parents were friends.

"Not Tiny Hurst," Lee insisted, her gaze gliding coolly over the lake, tracking the swans.

Nicole backed off at her irritated tone. Silent minutes passed as she ran through the lunchroom crowd, the football team, the basketball team, and the guys who spent the summer hanging around Lee's pool. Lee stretched out on her back, eyes closed, hands folded like those of a beautiful corpse. *Bored,* Nicole warned herself. *Think. Think fast!*

"Robbie Dougherty!" she cried suddenly. "He and Tanya broke up. Right after Halloween, remember? He's available."

"Robbie it is," Lee said. Her eyes remained closed, but a wicked little smile danced over her lips. "First thing Monday. Come prepared to take notes."

The place to find Robbie Dougherty first thing on a Monday or any other morning was the outdoor basketball court alongside the Oakview parking lot. Although Robbie wasn't on the team, he was a basketball addict. He toted a ball from his car to school every morning and back again every afternoon, just in case there were a few free minutes to take a couple of shots or hustle up a quick game of Horse. The ball stayed in his locker until lunch, which usually consisted of three minutes of gulping food followed by twenty-two minutes of shooting baskets—in the gym in bad weather, outside on the court in good.

Robbie had even been picked up by the Eli police one summer night in Truman Park, shooting baskets alone by the light of a streetlamp. There'd been complaints of drug dealing in the park, and a temporary curfew had been called. Robbie had nothing on him but shorts, sneakers, and sweat, so he got off with a warning.

His ex-girlfriend Tanya had spent most of the past year studying in empty bleachers or leaning against chain link fences behind goalposts. But when a spur-of-the-moment game in a junior high school yard left her waiting at home for an hour after her family had gone to her favorite cousin's wedding, the penalty was a returned friendship ring and goodbye.

Robbie wore the ring on his right pinky now, as he and a couple of freshmen tussled over a rebounding ball on Monday morning. Somehow Lee managed to be right where the ball landed in the grass after it was knocked out of bounds. She picked it up and held it in the crook of her arm so that Robbie had to come up really close to get it back.

"Lose something?" she asked and smiled up into his flushed face. The wink came next.

Robbie grinned down at her, breathing heavily for one reason or another, then squinted up toward the school as the first-hour warning bell sounded. "Game's over anyway," he said and made a dive for his books at the edge of the court. Lee held on to the ball.

They strolled up the steps together, Nicole trailing them, amazed at how easily Lee had made contact. Now Lee seemed to be having trouble walking in a straight line. She held the ball in her left arm, away from Robbie, and every other step brought a slight, but obvious, collision between some part of her body and a corresponding section of his.

He didn't object. And Lee seemed totally absorbed by whatever he was saying, which wasn't much, as far as Nicole could tell. It appeared fascinating to Lee, though, judging from her little noises of amusement and appreciation.

Once inside the building, Lee turned back just long enough to tell Nicole she'd see her at lunch—and to give a secretive but emphatic nod toward the row of lockers on her left, where Brian Marsh happened to be standing.

Ice water flooded Nicole's veins. As Brian slapped his

locker door shut and turned toward her, her heart threatened to freeze solid.

Somehow her mouth managed to open. "Hi, Brian," it said. Smile, she told herself. You have got to smile. Remember, you're doing him a big favor. A kind of spasm tore her lips apart and stretched them toward her ears.

Brian looked up from the books he was shuffling. "Oh, hi, Nicole," he said.

He knew her name! Lee was right. The smile made all the difference. What would the wink do? But when did it come in? She couldn't just suddenly wink out of nowhere, with no reason. She needed a cute or clever or sexy remark to go with it, like "Lose something?" Otherwise, he'd just think there was something wrong with her eye.

"How's it going?" Brian asked, wisps of sand-colored hair falling over his brow. When he looked up, the deep blue of his eyes invited her in for a swim.

How's what going? Nicole wondered. Say something. *Say something.* And get the dying cow look off your face. *Wink!*

"Not bad," she said.

And she winked. There! She was winking and smiling and talking! She was giving it everything she had.

At the sight of the wink, Brian grinned, a grin not unlike the grin Robbie had grinned at Lee. Contact!

"How about you?" she asked.

"If I make it through Spanish, I'll make it through the rest of my life," he said. "Which way are you walking?"

Don't blow it, Nicole warned herself. "Oh—ummm—"

"I go this way," Brian said, jerking his head to the right. "Second floor."

"Me, too." Nicole did not need to go anywhere near the second floor. She had gym, in the annex off the basement. She'd be very late. But it would be worth it.

"What's the big deal with Spanish?" she asked, fitting her step to Brian's.

"Teacher hates me."

"Why?"

"Says I have an attitude problem. Nothing wrong with my attitude. The foreign language requirement is a crock. My dad says they're just afraid to drop it, that's all, afraid some minority group'll go berserk at a school board meeting or something."

Nicole watched him out of the corner of her eye, hoping for a sign that he was kidding. But he was dead serious. He didn't even see anything the least bit stupid about what he was saying.

"Hey," he went on, obviously pleased with the point he was making, "if we're the greatest country in the world—and we are—everybody else should try to be more like us, right? Not the other way around. If you've got the best, why mess with the rest?"

The sparkling ocean Nicole had imagined in his eyes evaporated. The good-looking face grinning at her belonged to a bigoted jerk! Certainly not the only bigoted jerk in Eli, but what did falling for one of them make her? An idiot!

Nicole felt an urge to buy back her wink. In spite of the crowded hall, she made absolutely sure no part of her body touched anything belonging to Brian Marsh. At last, they reached the stairwell.

"I go down to the gym here," she said.

"Oh, okay. Nice talking to you."

"Right." Nicole sped down the stairs, trying to make up for the time she'd wasted.

She got to her gym locker just as the second bell rang. A couple of girls hurried past her and through the swinging doors to the gym, leaving the locker room empty. If she was lucky, Ms. Harris would be held up in her office blabbing to some jock from one of the girls' teams and wouldn't notice her mad dash onto the floor.

She ripped off her slacks and shirt and spun the combination of her lock. Of course, she was spinning the wrong numbers, the ones to her street locker. As she tried again, she thought she heard someone sniffling. She stopped fussing with the lock and listened.

It was coming from the next row, where a locker door suddenly banged shut. Nicole wrestled her limbs into her shorts and T-shirt. Just then, a body whooshed past her in the aisle between the rows of lockers.

"Tanya!" she gasped, in spite of herself. Tanya Breuer stopped short and turned a pair of red-rimmed eyes toward her. "Are you all right?"

Tanya shrugged. Her lower lip quivered. Nicole knew the feeling: If she opened her mouth to speak, she'd start to bawl. Tanya blinked hard several times. "We're late," she said at last and continued on toward the gym.

Nicole ran up the narrow aisle behind her. Should she ask about the tears? Or pretend she hadn't noticed anything? Was it any of her business? She and Tanya really didn't know each other all that well. They had a lot of the same classes and showed up at the same parties, but they'd never spent much time alone together. When Tanya wasn't with Robbie, she mostly hung out with Dawn Covington.

They reached the doors leading into the gym and pushed against them cautiously. Sure enough, a wall of noise hit them. Ms. Harris was nowhere to be seen, and a hundred girls in gym clothes were yakking away in untidy rows. Tanya and Nicole slid into line at the back of the room and sat cross-legged on the floor, side by side.

"I guess you heard me back there," Tanya said, nodding toward the locker room.

"Guess so."

"You know I broke up with Robbie."

Nicole nodded. Everybody knew that.

"Well, I shouldn't have," Tanya said. Tears immediately filled her eyes and choked off her words.

Nicole dug around in the pockets of her shorts and came up with a crumpled but reasonably clean tissue. Tanya took it, wiped away the mascara smudged under her eyes, and blew her nose.

"Robbie and I have been together since last Thanksgiving," she said. "It's our anniversary coming up—a whole year. How am I going to get through the holidays without him? How am I going to get through my life?"

Flabbergasted, Nicole glanced around the room for help. But the rest of the class were too busy gabbing to notice the drama in the back row. "Things'll work out," she found herself telling Tanya. "You'll find someone else."

What was she saying? She was the last one in the world to guarantee that!

Tanya sniffled. "I don't *want* anybody else. I want Robbie back, and I don't know what to do. Did you see him with Lee this morning? Doesn't she have enough boyfriends without taking mine?"

Nicole couldn't believe it. First the disappointment of Brian Marsh and now this. Ready to give up the game and confess everything, she was cut off by the shrill call of Ms. Harris's whistle. She scrambled to her feet and held out her hand to help Tanya.

On a platform at the front of the gym, Ms. Harris barked out her displeasure that the class had shown no initiative in getting the equipment out and instructed them to "Move it! Pronto!" Nicole and Tanya ambled toward the nearest low balance beam. By the time they reached it, Caroline Beck and her friend Brenda

Something-or-other—the brainy one—were already pulling it away from the wall and setting it in place. Nicole and Tanya stood together, arms folded, and watched Brenda totter across.

The urge to confess had passed. It was all too dreadful and embarrassing. "Can't you just talk to Robbie?" Nicole asked. "Offer to—you know—patch things up?"

"You don't know Robbie," Tanya said. "He's very sensitive. I mean, he was wrong to make me late for my cousin's wedding, but he admitted that, and I *still* said a bunch of stuff I shouldn't. Like how he wasn't on a basketball team, wasn't ever going to be on a basketball team, and looked like an ass running around with a ball under his arm all the time. It just came pouring out. I hated it even while I was saying it, but I couldn't stop. So he's hurt. And he doesn't get over things easily. He looks easygoing, but he's really kind of . . . fragile."

Nicole swallowed hard. She had to stop Lee before it was too late.

But it was lunch hour by the time she caught up with Lee outside the cafeteria. Yanking her back by the elbow, Nicole waved a cluster of freshmen on ahead of them through the doorway.

"Lee, I've got to talk to you," she said. "I want to call the whole thing off. You can't go on flirting with Robbie. Tanya wants him back."

"So let her take him back. I'm not stopping her," Lee said.

Nicole breathed a sigh of relief and followed Lee toward their usual table. "Fine," she said. "You should have seen Tanya in gym today. She's a wreck. She really loves him, you know?"

"If you say so," Lee replied, dropping her books on the table and heading back toward the food line. "How did it go with Brian Marsh?"

"I've changed my mind on that, too," Nicole said. "I mean, thanks anyway—and I've learned a lot. The smile works. The wink works. When I get a chance, I'll try the hip and shoulder moves. If I get a chance. If I ever meet a guy I want a chance with."

Lee raised an eyebrow, then shrugged. "Whatever," she said.

Nicole felt herself losing Lee's interest, slipping from favor, but it didn't much matter now. Tray loaded with pizza slices, carrot sticks, and a beige blob called a Dream Cookie, she trailed Lee back to the table.

Lee's usual seat awaited her. Beside it, a protective arm swung over the chairback, sat Robbie Dougherty. His face lit up as he spotted Lee approaching, and he gallantly swept a pile of books out of her way.

Shifting her tray to one hip, Nicole brought her face up close to Lee's. "All bets are off," she whispered. "You said Tanya could have him back."

"I said she could *take* him back," Lee corrected her. "I need help with trig and he's coming over tonight to study for the exam with me. Would the two of you like to join us?"

"Lee!" Nicole gasped. "This is not a joke—!"

"Neither is trig."

Lee slipped into the seat beside Robbie's.

Nicole's heart sank. She found a seat near the end of the long double table, across from Stacey Lawrence.

"Something wrong?" Stacey asked.

"No," Nicole replied. "Nothing. I'm fine."

She wished she could confide in Stacey, talk about Lee's power over people, explain how she'd gotten Robbie involved and how much she regretted it. But she'd sound like a complete fool if she admitted her own part in what was happening, and she had the feeling lately that Stacey already thought she had club soda where her brains should be.

They'd been best friends forever, but lately they'd drifted apart. With Stacey away all summer, Nicole had naturally grown closer to Lee. And Stacey had changed so much over the summer, she made Nicole feel awkward and shy. Stacey was a senior the way Nicole thought seniors should be: past all the petty teenage stuff, full of plans and confidence. By comparison, Nicole seemed to be getting younger and dumber and more confused by the minute. This last fiasco was not going to earn her any points with Stacey. Better just to keep her mouth shut.

The week passed, with Robbie at Lee's house every evening and close by her side at school. He didn't even take off for the basketball court the minute he'd gulped down his lunch. Tanya's harangue had affected him—to Lee's benefit, not Tanya's. Nicole kept her distance from all three of them, especially Tanya, who looked more haggard with each passing day.

Thanksgiving came and went, with too many relatives and too much food, as usual. Plus something new this year, too many questions: No plans for college yet? No boyfriend yet? No future yet? What are you waiting for?

Nicole was feeling only relief as she pulled her car into the school lot, the holiday turmoil finally behind her. The *whack* of a ball hitting concrete took her by surprise as it drew her attention to the basketball court. There was Robbie, alone, dribbling and shooting with a vengeance, a dark scowl on his face. She'd almost forgotten about him!

But this was not the usual Robbie-plus-basketball picture of bliss. He was upset. And neither Lee nor Tanya was in sight.

Once inside the building, Nicole stashed her books in

her own locker and hurried to Lee's to see if she could catch her before class. Lee was there, peeling off her jacket.

"Hi, Nicole," she said, flashing her lovely smile. "I thought about you this weekend. Craig and Ray were in town. I fixed Cassie Daniels up with Ray. We had a blast!"

"What about Robbie?" Nicole asked.

Lee brushed her hair, eyeing herself in a small mirror hung inside her locker from the vents in the door. "Oh, well, that's over. I mean, it wasn't real anyway, was it? Not real enough to give up a weekend with Craig, that's for sure. Anyway, Robbie and I both aced the trig exam, so it worked out okay."

"Didn't he kind of expect to see you this weekend? What did you tell him?"

"I told him I was busy. He caught on fast."

"He's very sensitive," Nicole muttered.

A group of girls closed in around Lee as she kicked her locker shut and tucked the brush into her purse. "How's Craig, Lee?" one of the girls sang out, and the others dissolved into giggles. Lee launched into the story of her cadet weekend as she led the group down the hall.

Nicole watched them go. Suddenly she knew what Lee had, what made it all so easy for her. *She didn't care.* There was no way to get at Lee, to hurt her, to *win*, because she simply did not care. That gave her power no one else had.

The Ice Queen. Tiny Hurst was right. And that was why Lee said he wasn't her type. He understood her games too well, and he would never fall for them.

Nicole took a deep breath and let it out slowly. She had no talent for games. She understood that now. But that was fine because she no longer wanted to play. She glanced up and down the hall quickly, looking for Stacey. They needed to talk.

WINTER

BLIND DATING

"Hello? Anybody home? Oh, here you are!"

Dawn Covington snapped awake, her heart racing. The hulking figure in the archway between the living and dining rooms came slowly into focus as Tanya Breuer, wrapped in her winter coat and watching Dawn with amusement. "Oh," Dawn said, "it's only you."

Her biology textbook lay spread-eagle beside the sofa, its pages crumpled under the heavy cover. She scooped it up and licked the dryness from her mouth as she tried to smooth the creased pages. It took a long time for the thudding in her chest to quiet down.

"Well, gee, thanks." Tanya peeled off her coat and gloves and flopped onto a wing-back chair near the tall front windows. "You really know how to make a pal feel welcome."

"I meant it's only you and not my mom. What time is it?"

"Nearly six."

"Nearly six? Are you kidding?" Dawn jumped to her feet and frantically gathered her books, pen, and notes together. "I haven't even started dinner!" Patting everything into a reasonably neat pile on the coffee table, she took off for the kitchen.

Tanya followed close behind her. "Relax, will you? Your mom isn't even here yet. Can't you just nuke something for her?"

"Well, I'll have to, won't I?" Dawn rummaged through a wooden cabinet and retrieved large cans of Campbell's Chicken Noodle soup and Progresso Ham and Bean. "This'll have to do," she mumbled, balancing a can in each hand and examining the labels. "I wonder where Mom is? She's usually home from work by now."

Suddenly her head popped up and she faced Tanya squarely. "What are you doing here, anyway? How'd you get in?"

Tanya crossed her arms in mock dismay. "Finally woke up, did you? Your back door was open. Not a great idea, by the way. Eli may not be St. Louis yet, but it's not Walton's Mountain anymore, either. And there you were, a sleeping duck."

Dawn shrugged and set the cans on the counter. She'd let her mother decide between them when she got home. "I was studying for that biology lab exam tomorrow. Or at least I was trying to. Every time I read one page, I fall asleep."

Tanya dropped into a chair at the kitchen table, her dark eyes bright with excitement. "Forget the biology exam," she said. "What are you doing Friday night?"

"Friday?" Dawn asked hesitantly. "I don't know. Why?"

"Do you want to go on a blind date? Let me rephrase that. You have *got* to go on a blind date. This guy is visiting Robbie—a friend he used to know at camp. His name is Kevin. It'll be kind of a three-way reunion celebration! Robbie and me, Robbie and his friend, and you and me double-dating again."

Dawn shot a glance at the clock over the sink. Where was her mother? "I can't," she told Tanya.

"What do you mean you can't?" Tanya scowled. "Dawn, you're not listening to me. I've met this person. He is *really* cute. And I don't just mean good-looking cute. I mean funny and sweet and whatever else you have on your ten-most-wanted-in-a-date list. *Plus* he's a sophomore in college. Did you know some college kids get a month off for

51

Christmas break? Can you believe that? Man, I can't wait to get there."

"Leave it to you to go to college for the vacations."

Tanya flipped her thick, straw-colored French braid over her shoulder. "Yeah, well, that's for next year. What about Friday?"

"I can't, Tanya. Maybe some other time."

Tanya leaped to her feet and all but danced around the kitchen with impatience. "Oh, come on, Dawn. It's Christmas. Get with the spirit."

"It's not Christmas yet. Christmas is when we get to study for midterms. We're still only up to the lab exam, thank goodness."

Tanya fell back into her chair and groaned. "Midterms. How boring. Besides, they're nearly a month away."

"These are the grades colleges look at," Dawn reminded her. "Not our finals. They've already made their decisions by then. This is it. You may not need financial aid, but I do."

"Is one Friday night going to make such a big difference?" Tanya asked. Suddenly her round face lit up with inspiration. "We'll go Christmas shopping, the four of us. That'll be practical, but fun. You have to go Christmas shopping, don't you?" She fluttered her hands in the air. "The decorations are up. Santa's little elves and all. The carols are playing."

"Oh, spare me!" Dawn cried. "I work at the mall, remember? I helped put up those decorations. That music is already driving me crazy—"

Tanya's face fell and her hands dropped into her lap. "Oh, yeah. So we'll do something else."

"I can't," Dawn insisted. "My mom needs me. She likes to relax on Friday nights—rent a movie, pop some popcorn. Fridays are practically the only time we have together."

"So how about we just go for yogurt after school tomor-row?" Tanya suggested. "You can at least say hello."

"I have to shop for groceries after school."

"Oh, for crying out loud, Dawn, what has gotten into you lately? You have the rest of your life to shop for groceries."

"And I have to make dinner."

"Ahhhhgh!" Tanya wailed. "I cannot believe you are doing this to me. I've already told Kevin all about you!"

"Tanya—"

"Okay, okay. How about tonight then? We could run by for a couple of hours—or you could come over to my house. Just give him a chance—"

"You know we have that lab exam tomorrow."

"You are turning into a real drudge, Dawn Covington, you know that? This is your *senior year*. One senior year to a customer."

"That's why I'm studying so hard for this exam," Dawn pointed out.

"That's why you're supposed to be having *fun*," Tanya shot back.

Dawn's patience ran out. There didn't seem to be any way she could make Tanya understand what was impor-tant and what was not important in her life right now.

"I didn't plan for my senior year to turn out this way," she snapped, feeling the tension grip her jaws as she spoke. "It just did. I wish it could be different, but it isn't, so I have to live with it."

Immediately, Tanya's broad face softened with sympa-thy. "Oh, Dawn, I'm sorry. I know things have been rough for you and your mom. I didn't mean to make them worse. I just thought—you know—"

Outside, the garage door squealed open on its rollers. Dawn glanced out the window in time to see her mother's Honda pull in.

53

"Cool it," she told Tanya. "My mom's home. So—thanks for asking, but no thanks." She maneuvered toward the living room and Tanya's coat, drawing Tanya along with her. "Listen, I'll see you in biology tomorrow, okay? Are you ready for the test?"

Tanya's head bounced gaily as she bundled up. "Oh, sure. I could flunk it with my eyes closed."

They returned to the kitchen just as Mrs. Covington came through the back door, purse in one hand, briefcase in the other. "Oh, hi, Tanya!" she cried. "How are you? Are you leaving already? I haven't seen you in ages."

"Hi, Mrs. Covington. Yeah, well, I guess we've all been kind of busy."

"Don't I know it?" Mrs. Covington agreed. "Excuse me, girls, I have got to get these shoes off."

"Sure, Mom."

"See you, Mrs. Covington."

Dawn waved Tanya out the door, then followed her mother into the living room.

"After six already," Mrs. Covington said, then groaned and let her briefcase drop to the floor as she sank into an easy chair. She kicked off her black pumps and rubbed one slender foot against the arch of the other as she unbuttoned her jacket. "Client would not stop talking. Told him I had a class tonight. Told him I had exactly one hour between the time I get home—well, normally get home—and the time I have to be in class. He found that very interesting. Told me all about the class he was taking in genealogy. Turns out he can—and did—trace his entire family all the way back to the *Mayflower*. At least he thinks it's his family. There are many branches on the Thompson tree. Oh, why am I telling you this? Who cares?" Mrs. Covington paused and sniffed the air. "Do I smell something cooking?"

"No," Dawn admitted. "I have this killer lab exam tomorrow and I was trying so hard to cram it all in, I fell asleep. Then Tanya stopped by. I'm sorry. I'll get something started."

Mrs. Covington let her head fall back against the tufted chair. "That's all right," she said. "I'm too tired to eat anyway."

"You have to eat," Dawn said. "You have three hours of class to go. You need your energy."

"I suppose," Mrs. Covington agreed, sinking deeper into the chair.

"I'll just heat up a can of soup," Dawn offered, starting back toward the kitchen. "Chicken noodle or ham and bean?"

"No beans before a three-hour class," Mrs. Covington called after her.

Dawn giggled. "Okay. We have those sourdough rolls you like. And I bought Sara Lee snack cakes. The chocolate ones."

Seconds later, Mrs. Covington appeared in the kitchen doorway, shoes in one hand, briefcase in the other. "Chocolate and you, babe," she said, her face crinkling in a weary smile, "make everything else bearable."

Dawn answered her mother's smile with one of her own. "In that order?" she asked.

"Not necessarily."

Suddenly feeling shy, Dawn turned her attention to opening the can of soup and dumping it into a large glass casserole dish. When she looked up again, her mother was gone.

She'd be back when the soup and rolls were ready, looking as fantastic in her school clothes, as she called them— slacks and sweater—as she had in her business suit and pumps. By day, she worked for an accounting firm. By night, she was taking courses toward a master's degree in business. No one Dawn knew had a mother quite like hers—pretty, smart, funny, and so with it, she seemed more like a friend or a sister than a mother.

And no one Dawn knew could figure out why Dawn's father had left her, nearly seven months ago, just after Dawn's junior year. Oh, she and her mom had discussed it, of course; they discussed everything. She and her dad had even had a talk, formal as a summit conference, before he took off for the West Coast. But all the words that passed among them didn't seem to add up to anything that made sense to Dawn.

"I have to find myself," her father had said over a cheese-and-broccoli-stuffed baked potato at the mall food court. He'd chosen the place for their chat. It was somewhere neutral, Dawn figured, like Switzerland. Somewhere nice and public where she couldn't throw a fit.

Did he know how stupid he sounded, spouting clichés like some airhead in a soap opera?

"You're not lost," she'd told him. The bacon bits on her own potato tasted like sawdust. She went on eating anyway, grinding her teeth in anger.

"I am," he'd insisted. "Or something is. Something in my life is missing, Dawn. I can't expect you to understand. You're too young. But maybe you will one day, and you'll forgive me."

His fair-lashed brown eyes held hers for a long time. He was a handsome man, her father, red-haired, charming, and used to getting his own way. There was a time when Dawn would have done anything for his smile. Even as a child, she sensed that everyone he met felt the same way.

But not now. "Maybe," she'd said, breaking away from his gaze to pick at her food.

And so they'd parted, quietly, grimly, with no tears and

no big scene. He'd even told her how much he appreci-ated that, how it made it so much easier on everyone. Everyone? Ha!

"Your father has a clock inside of him," her mother had tried to explain, "and it's set in perfect synchrony with the baby boom generation."

They were sitting on the edge of Dawn's bed, a couple of weeks after he'd gone. Her mother kept wanting to talk about it, in her calm, reasonable way. Dawn couldn't ask her not to, not when her mother was being so brave and practical and supportive. But it was easier for Dawn to stay strong if she stayed angry, her anger wrapped around her like a suit of armor.

"When it was time to go to San Francisco and wear flowers in your hair," Mrs. Covington went on, "he was in the first wave out. When it was time to pack away the sandals and make it big in a business suit, he beat every-one else to the top. And now, it must be time to have a midlife crisis."

"Meaning what?" Dawn had asked.

"Meaning stop whatever you're doing and do the oppo-site, I suppose."

"How can you stop being a father?"

Mrs. Covington had let the back of her hand slide gently along Dawn's cheek. Standing alone at the sink now, measuring out a can of water for the soup, Dawn could almost call back the softness of her touch and the faint sweetness of her hand lotion. She shuddered, shak-ing the memory away, and concentrated on setting the microwave timer.

"Soup's on," she yelled toward the stairwell a few min-utes later, as she ladled equal portions of chicken, noodles, and broth into two bowls. Before Dawn had carried the second bowl to the table, her mother breezed in, hurrying

57

toward the refrigerator. She looked fresh again, in her forest green sweater and slacks, and her light brown hair smelled of orange blossoms.

"Chicken soup," she observed, carrying margarine for their rolls and milk for their coffee to the table. "Good for what ails you."

They were cooling down their first spoonfuls when the phone rang.

"I'll get it," Dawn said. "You eat. It's almost time for you to go." She plucked the receiver off the wall phone in the middle of the second ring.

At the other end of the line, Tanya skipped "hello" and got right to the point: "I just want to say I'm sorry if I bugged you too much or hurt your feelings."

"Oh, Tanya, it's okay. Really."

"And I also want to know if you're absolutely, positively sure you don't want to go out Friday."

"Tanya, please—"

"Think prom date, Dawn. It's not that far away. Think New Year's Eve. And the Sweetheart Dance. This is an investment. Kevin's at Southwest State, only an hour away. It's perfect. And if you don't take him, Cassie Daniels will."

Dawn's voice hardened. "Tanya. I am not interested."

"Sigh. Double sigh. Gulp. What a waste."

"Goodbye, Tanya."

"Bye."

Mrs. Covington was on her feet now, stuffing a bite of roll into her mouth as she hurried out of the room to get her books. Half her dinner was still on the table. Dawn hung up the receiver and removed the Sara Lee cakes from the freezer.

Mrs. Covington bustled into the kitchen again and dropped her books on the counter with a thud. "Anything important?" she asked, charging across the room to retrieve her purse from the back of a chair.

"No, it was just Tanya."

"She and Robbie on the blink again?"

"No, they're together. He was sorry, she was sorry, and all was forgiven. They're fine."

Slowing down the search in her purse for her car keys, Mrs. Covington cocked her head to one side to look at Dawn. "I haven't seen much of Tanya lately," she said. "Come to think of it, I haven't seen any of your friends."

Dawn squirmed out from under her mother's gaze by fussing with the box of Sara Lee cakes. "Been busy, I guess."

Mrs. Covington's head bobbed in agreement as she speeded up again. At last, balancing keys, purse, and books, she yanked open the back door. "Aren't we all?" she mused. "Busy, busy, busy."

Dawn dropped an individually wrapped chocolate cake into her mother's gaping purse. "Quick energy," she said.

"Chocolate and you, babe," her mother replied and propelled herself outside, blowing Dawn a quick kiss. "See you at ten. Better get back to your frog livers or whatever. And thanks for dinner. Did we eat dinner? Yes, well, almost. Bye."

For a moment, the sound of her voice and the smell of her perfume lingered in the air. Then the house was deadly still again. You can always tell when you're alone in a house, Dawn thought. Even when someone's in a room at the other end, you can feel it. Empty feels different.

She flipped on the radio beside her mother's drooping African violet on the counter and let an interview with a singer she'd never heard of blast the silence around her as she ate her lukewarm soup and roll. Then she took her coffee to the sink with her and sipped it as she washed and dried the other dishes. After refilling her cup and carrying the radio into the living room, she settled back on the sofa, biology notes propped on her knees.

Between the coffee and the classic rock following the interview, she managed to stay awake and get her studying done—or at least as done as it would ever be. This was only a lab exam, she reminded herself. As Tanya had so cheerfully pointed out, midterms were nearly a month away.

Mrs. Covington dragged in promptly at ten, yawning noisily. Dawn made room for her on the sofa, and the two of them watched Jason Daniels read the news on Channel 10.

"Cassie says he's been offered a better job in Indianapolis," Dawn told her mother. "They're moving in a couple of months."

"Hmmmmm." Mrs. Covington stifled another yawn. "Must be hard on Cassie, switching schools all the time. Especially now, in the middle of her senior year."

Dawn shrugged. "At least her whole family goes together."

Mrs. Covington wrapped Dawn in a one-armed hug without saying anything. They watched the weather forecast, then straggled off to their own rooms to get ready for bed.

The room was dark when Dawn suddenly found herself sitting bolt upright in bed. It seemed as if she'd been asleep for hours, but the numbers on her digital clock glowed at 11:48. What had awakened her? She listened to the night sounds in her room—the hum of the furnace fan, an occasional creak and groan as the December cold pressed against the walls and windows.

There was something else. Dawn slipped out of bed and

padded across the carpeted floor to the hall, where the sound grew louder. She followed it to her mother's closed bedroom door. A rim of light was visible around the frame, where the door had pulled away as the old house settled. She knocked. A moment passed before her mother answered. "Yes? Come on in."

Nothing could have prepared Dawn for the sight of her mother's glistening eyes and the pale yellow tissues crumpled up on the blanket.

"What's the matter?" she asked.

The hush of her own voice, the shadowy room, and the strange night quiet reminded her of a time very long ago, when she was little. She'd gone through a period when she'd been afraid to fall asleep. She was convinced that unless she stayed awake and stood guard, night creatures would steal away everything she loved. Nothing her parents did or said could comfort her or change her mind. Eventually, she'd outgrown her fears—or maybe she'd just gotten too tired to stay awake anymore. What she was feeling now, watching her mother's haggard face in the pool of lamplight, seemed awfully familiar.

Mrs. Covington gathered up a handful of used tissues and tossed them onto her night table, then patted the blanket for Dawn to sit down. Dawn sank onto the bed, facing her, waiting for some explanation, or better yet, a magic spell that would bring her calm, capable, funny mother back again and take this strange, troubled woman away.

Mrs. Covington opened her mouth to speak, then clamped it shut and regarded Dawn with moist, pain-filled eyes while she swallowed the tears holding back her voice.

"I think," she said finally, in a hoarse whisper, "that I am very, very tired."

"Is that all?"

"Tonight, that's all." Mrs. Covington pulled another tissue out of the box beside her on the bed, wiped her eyes with it, and blew her nose.

"What do you mean, tonight?" Dawn asked.

"On other nights, I've cried for other reasons. Anger. Loneliness. Fear. Self-pity—that's always a big one. Tonight, I think it's just exhaustion."

"I can't believe I've never heard you before," Dawn said.

Mrs. Covington reached out to give Dawn's hand a comforting pat. "Oh, don't worry about it, babe. I'm all right. Really, I am."

Dawn was not convinced. "How can I not worry about you crying all by yourself in the middle of the night?"

"There are worse things than tears, Dawn," her mother insisted. "And once you've had a good cry, you know, things generally do start to pick up."

Mrs. Covington opened her arms and Dawn let herself be drawn in for a hug.

"See?" her mother said. "You cry a little; you hug a little. Things pick up. And now, we'd both better get some sleep."

"Are you sure you're all right?"

Mrs. Covington's smile already had some of its sparkle back. "I'm sure. Thank you for caring, babe."

Once back in her own bed, Dawn took a long time to fall asleep. She kept thinking she could still hear her mother crying. Twice she tiptoed out into the hall, once all the way to her mother's door, even though there was no light shining around the edges. Her mother was asleep now, sure, but she'd been awake, tonight and who knows how many other nights? The thought filled Dawn with terror.

Of course, she'd been stupid to think her mother *hadn't* cried, not once in the seven months since her father had gone. How could she have imagined that the glittering daytime person was all there was to her? Busy, busy, busy—that was how her mother got through the days, and that was all she let anyone else see. . . .

Eventually, Dawn fell asleep, but the night was filled with frightening dreams. When her alarm went off in the morning, she couldn't remember any of them, but the feeling of dread lingered all day. She blamed it on the biology exam.

For the rest of the week, Dawn found herself peering at her mother out of the corner of her eye every minute they were together, checking for signs of unhappiness, for a crack in her amazing strength. Each glimpse of a smile, each shared joke, would relieve her fearfulness for a while, but then it would start all over again—the building anxiety, the search for reassurance.

"Is something bothering you?" her mother asked over a stir-fried vegetable dish she'd made that Friday night. She had no classes on Friday evenings, so it was her turn to cook.

Dawn shook her head hard. Mrs. Covington looked doubtful but went on nibbling her snow peas.

For a few minutes, neither spoke. Even that troubled Dawn. In the little time they had together, she and her mother were rarely quiet. A Friday night conversation could go anywhere: politics, money, movie stars.

Finally Mrs. Covington put down her fork and pushed herself back from the table. "I've got something to tell you, babe," she said. "There's this man—he seems to be a very nice guy—in one of my classes. I've chatted with him several times during our breaks. Anyway, last night he invited me to a Christmas party. It's next Friday."

Dawn felt the floor fall away from under her chair. "Fridays are *ours*," she said.

Her mother seemed surprised. "We've had lots of them," she said. "And we'll have plenty more. It's just—"

"And a *Christmas* party? Isn't this Christmas going to be rotten enough?"

"But that's why—" her mother began.

"I could have gone out tonight, you know," Dawn interrupted, as a surge of anger swept away the weightless feeling. "Remember when Tanya called earlier this week? That was about a blind date. But I said no because we always spend Fridays together. *Alone*, together."

"Always?"

Dawn met her mother's quizzical glance, then looked away. "Ever since . . . since Daddy left."

"Well, that's not always," Mrs. Covington said. "Before last summer, you were out more Fridays than you were home. And Saturdays and Sundays and sometimes weekdays, too. And now you never go out at all, unless I suggest we go somewhere. How come?"

"What do you mean, how come?" Dawn yelped. What was she being accused of? *She* wasn't the one wandering off with strangers. "I go to school on the weekdays and work on the weekends. I do the shopping. I cook dinner almost every night. I clean up after dinner. I run the laundry during the week. I do everything I can to help you. And now you're making me feel as if that's *wrong*."

Dawn's voice rose with every word, try as she might to control it, until it reached an infantile squeal and finally came to a stop.

"I appreciate everything you do," Mrs. Covington said calmly. "I thank my lucky stars every day that I have you. You know that, don't you?"

"I guess so."

"You guess so? Haven't I told you? Haven't I shown you? You're the most precious thing in the world to me, babe. I don't think I've ever kept that a secret. Have I?"

Biting her lip to keep it from quivering, Dawn shook her head.

"Okay," her mother said. "So does my going out one Friday change anything?"

Dawn's fist hit the table. "Yes!" she cried. "I've done everything I could think of to help you, and now you're just going on with your own life as if I didn't matter."

"I never asked you to give up *your* life, Dawn," Mrs. Covington insisted. "Is that why I haven't seen Tanya or any of your friends over here for months? Did you think giving up your friends would help *me?*"

"I wanted to be here for you," Dawn said.

"That's very admirable," her mother observed.

But her face was dark, and somehow the word *admirable* struck Dawn like a blow. She slumped back in her chair. Okay, so maybe part of her *had* wanted to seem admirable—the noble daughter supporting her stricken mother. And maybe that was dumb. But it wasn't the only reason she'd cut herself off from everything to stay home. And it wasn't the reason she'd been watching her mother every waking moment for signs of weakness—and listening for her tears in the middle of the night. Even now, she couldn't resist a sidelong glance at her mother's face, a reading of her mood. What she saw scared her. "Don't look at me like that," she pleaded.

"Like what?" Mrs. Covington asked, the dark expression immediately giving way to confusion.

"Like you hate me," Dawn said.

"Why would I hate you?" her mother exclaimed. "How

could I ever hate you? What are you talking about? What is going on?"

Dawn stared at the water chestnuts and onions congealing in their sauce in front of her. On either side of her plate were her own hands, clenched into fists. She was terrified. Her mother was all she had left. There was nothing and no one else in the entire world to care about or trust. If I lose you, she thought, not daring to say it out loud, not even sure she knew how . . .

She could discuss anything and everything with her mother, except this. There were no words for it. It seemed to come from a part of her that had existed before language. Babe. Baby. Baby me. Hold me. Tight.

She looked up. Her mother was still waiting for the words that weren't there. Their eyes met over the silence. Mrs. Covington reached across the table and covered Dawn's clenched hands with her own graceful fingers.

"I refuse to let you use me as an excuse to hide out here, Dawn."

"I'm not hiding out," Dawn insisted. "I'm . . . I'm standing guard."

At last, the tears fell. There was no denying them. She'd been standing guard all her life, and it didn't help. Nothing helped. What the night creatures wanted, they took.

"I haven't seen you cry in all these months," Mrs. Covington observed quietly.

"I haven't," Dawn said, pulling herself upright and trying to gather the fragments of her armor around her.

"Maybe it's time you got to it," Mrs. Covington suggested. "And got it over with."

Dawn pressed a napkin to her face, but the tears soon drenched right through it. "I miss him," she murmured, hating the words and herself for admitting them.

"I know," her mother said. "So do I."

Dawn held her breath for a moment until the sobbing finally stopped, then wiped her eyes and nose and shook her head wearily. It was all too confusing, too painful. Anger was so much simpler, and it got you straight through the day. "Why do I still love him?" she asked. "He doesn't deserve it. I wish I could stop. He doesn't even write or call."

Mrs. Covington smiled ruefully. "Don't be sorry you love someone, babe. Just be glad you're the kind of person who can. Not everyone has that gift." She leaned forward and brushed back a curl sticking to Dawn's wet cheek. "Who is this guy Tanya wanted to fix you up with?" she asked.

Dawn shrugged. "Friend of Robbie's."

"Nice?"

"She says so."

"Is it too late to call her?"

"Don't want to."

"Maybe you'll like him."

"Don't want to."

"Don't want to what? Call? Or like him?"

"Both."

"We've got to learn to trust people again, Dawn. We've been hurt, you and I, but it's time to try again."

"Can't."

"Can and must and will," Mrs. Covington insisted. "Life goes on, and I don't want to miss it. Do you?"

"Life hurts."

"Yes, it does. Sometimes. It's all a blind date, isn't it? Every day, every minute, you open the door and see what shows up."

"Even you and me? We're not a blind date."

"Aren't we new to each other this very moment?" Mrs.

Covington asked. "Wasn't I new to you when you caught me crying the other night?"

Dawn shuddered. New, yes. And scary.

"I distinctly remember holding this blanketed bug in my arms and thinking, Dawn Alicia Covington, who *are* you? I keep finding out, every day."

"I'm your daughter," Dawn said. "And Daddy's daughter, too, whether or not he cares to remember that."

"And Tanya's friend," her mother went on, taking Dawn's hands in her own again. "And a senior at Oakview High School. And a salesperson at the mall on weekends. And maybe some lucky guy's date."

"Not yet. Not tonight."

"Don't wait too long, babe."

Dawn felt her fists relax under her mother's warm grasp. They wove their fingers together and exchanged shy smiles. There was so much to think about. After the night creatures, then what? Maybe when you woke up the next morning—if you did wake up, if you made yourself open your eyes—a new life could be waiting to take the old one's place. Maybe.

"So—what are you thinking about now?" Mrs. Covington asked.

"I'm thinking—" Dawn said. "I'm thinking it's time for dessert."

"You are?"

"Yes, I am."

"Well," Mrs. Covington said, "there happens to be a box of tiny chocolate Santas I was saving. . . ."

"Now," Dawn said.

"Now," her mother agreed.

Dawn held a chair steady while her mother teetered on top of it and dug toward the back of a high cabinet shelf. "And a Merry Christmas to us!" Mrs. Covington announced as the red and green package emerged from its hiding place.

"Chocolate and you make everything else bearable," Dawn told her.

"In that order?"

"Not necessarily."

FIRST NIGHT

"Jeez, Hightower, get out of the car already," Tiny pleaded from the driver's seat. "Before somebody discovers our frozen corpses."

"Is it my fault your heater's busted?" Walt snapped at the reflection of Tiny's eyes in the rearview mirror. On the first syllable of *heater*, his voice took off like a misguided missile, collided with high C, then plummeted toward a gravelly whimper. Blood rushed to his cheeks at the pitiful sound.

As he attempted to extricate himself from the backseat of Tiny Hurst's creaking Ford wagon, he discovered yet another problem: His hands were suddenly too big. His fingers seemed swollen and numb as he struggled to get his gloves off to unlock the door. Nicole finally had to swivel around in the front seat and pull up the little whatchamacallit for him with her fuzzy-mittened hand.

"You want me to run up and get her?" she asked.

"I could just blow the horn," Tiny put in.

"No," Walt told them. "I'll do it. I'll get her. I'm going."

Now there was the door handle to wrestle with, first with his gloves on, then with them off, right hand, left hand.

Watching him over the seat back, Nicole laughed. "It's not as if this were a real date, Walt," she said. "There's nothing to be nervous about."

"I'm not nervous," Walt muttered, then shouldered the door open with such force he nearly threw himself out into the snow.

How is it possible, he wondered, for someone as smart as I'm supposed to be—and we're talking skip-fifth-grade-and-go-straight-into-middle-school here, we're talking sixteen-year-old high school senior, we're talking National Merit Scholarship finalist—how can someone that smart be such a total idiot?

He was, of course, nervous. He knew it; Nicole knew it. Possibly, it had made the six o'clock news. And now his feet were too big. The sight of his gigantic boots moving in slow motion up the snowdrifted path to Stacey's house nearly made him ill with anxiety. Okay, so it wasn't a real date. But it was New Year's Eve with Stacey Lawrence, something he'd been fantasizing about since seventh grade.

The porch light over her front door made the snow-covered lawn sparkle. Delicate tree branches sheathed in ice surrounded him with their glitter. Lugging his huge hands and feet along, he seemed to be entering a weird dream—not exactly a nightmare, but not quite the happy fantasy he'd had in mind either. In the fantasy version of this scene, he'd always been a lot older, and taller, and worldly wise—everything he was not in real life. For six-teen long years, he'd been playing catch-up on a wildly lopsided field. The youngest of four children at home, he was way ahead scholastically at school, but he couldn't even get into the game socially. He had a perfect, straight-A average, and he was still the class mascot, everybody's baby-faced, computer-brained kid brother.

Tonight had to be different.

He stamped his boots loudly on the mat in front of Stacey's door, and the sound struck him as ominous and all too real. He was actually about to ring her doorbell. He would press his finger—his suddenly overlarge and clumsy finger—on the button wired to electric chimes inside her house, and she would appear in the doorway and come out into the night with him. He would have to think of things to say to her. He would also have to think of things to say to her parents.

71

But first, he needed to go ahead and ring the stupid bell. Somehow, he managed it. Stacey opened the door herself; greeted him with an odd, strained smile; and drew him into the blinding light and smothering warmth of her living room.

"Mom, Dad, you remember Walt Hightower," she announced flatly.

Mr. and Mrs. Lawrence glanced in his direction from easy chairs facing each other across the fireplace. Their smiles of greeting were even more sickly than Stacey's.

Have I done something wrong? Walt wondered. I just got here. What could I have done? He felt himself go light-headed.

"I'll get my jacket," Stacey said.

Do not leave this room, Walt begged her silently. But it was a short trip into the dining room, where he could see her jacket draped over a chair. Even unstrung, he was still able to admire the swing of her dark hair as she walked and the way her jeans fit perfectly into the tops of her boots—and everywhere else. The loose-fitting beige sweater she wore made her look sexy and childlike, both at once, and very cuddly.

He sighed. Then, catching himself reflected in Mr. Lawrence's glinting eyes, he tried desperately not to think about Stacey's jeans anymore.

Now she was beside him, turning up the collar of her down-filled green jacket. Perfume drifted toward him each time she moved, and he wondered how his weakened knees would ever get his humongous feet back down the porch stairs. Stacey tucked her arm into his, almost as if to assist him, and he was grateful.

"Bye," she told her parents, without actually looking at them. She yanked the front door open and headed straight for the porch. "Don't wait up."

"Don't *make* us wait up," Mr. Lawrence growled.

"Happy New Year," Walt tried to toss in, as Stacey hauled him outside after her. There was a weak reply from Mrs. Lawrence, and in Walt's last glimpse of her before Stacey pulled the door shut, she seemed on the verge of tears.

Sweat stung Walt's armpits in spite of the cold biting at his face. Still tucked right up close to his side as they hurried toward Tiny's car, Stacey bent her head to avoid the fairyland branches, and her hair brushed Walt's cheek, sending another whiff of perfume his way and rivulets of sweat down the insides of his shirt.

"Did I do something wrong in there?" he asked.

"No."

"So what's up?"

"Nothing." Stacey tumbled into the backseat of Tiny's wagon. "I don't want to talk about it."

"About what?" Tiny asked as Walt folded and stuffed himself in beside Stacey.

"Nothing. It's nothing. Forget it." Stacey forced a perky smile onto her face to prove her point. "Happy New Year, everybody. Can we just have some fun?"

"Okay!" Nicole agreed for all of them and bounced around on her seat to face forward again. "Downtown, James," she commanded.

"The name's Keith," Tiny said. "Tiny, to my friends. You may call me Mr. Hurst."

Nicole giggled and moved closer to him. "I'm freezing to death, Mr. Hurst."

"I could fix that," Tiny offered, and Nicole laughed again. The wagon remained inert, its windows fogged over.

Walt glanced at Stacey. She was scrunched against the side door, arms folded, thoughts already somewhere else, probably back on the "nothing" she didn't want to talk about. He checked his watch.

"If we're going to have fun," he said, "we better have it fast. I have to meet Jamie and the guys at nine-fifteen, the latest. Our set starts at nine-thirty."

Stacey snapped out of her funk. "Oh, Walt, I completely forgot! You're going to play tonight—in front of the whole city. That's so exciting!"

"In front of whoever shows up," Walt said, struggling to maintain his cool in spite of the welcome burst of enthusiasm. "This whole thing could be a bust."

"No, it won't," Nicole assured him. "I've been talking it up all over school. And there's been tons of First Night publicity on TV and in the paper."

"Yah," Walt agreed, "but there are tons of other things to see and do during our time slot. And Mushroom Cloud is not exactly a household name outside Oakview High."

"Tonight, Eli, tomorrow, the world!" Tiny said, finally getting the Ford in gear and coaxing it over icy ruts toward the corner. "Assuming we ever get off this block."

The sudden cold snap and snowstorm were not what the Downtown Eli Business Association had had in mind when they'd planned the First Night celebration. The big hope was that opening all the buildings around the public square for New Year's Eve and bringing in every kind of food and entertainment they could gather would breathe life back into the old neighborhood.

The event was being billed as chemical-free, so hard-line revelers would probably stay away. There wouldn't even be any smoking allowed inside the buildings. But whole families could party together, even with little kids, and bands like Mushroom Cloud, too young to play the local bars, could have their first public performance.

And Stacey had forgotten Walt would be a part of it.

That figured. The band had been playing school parties and talent shows practically since the gang was spin the bottle age, and hardly anyone in the class noticed Walt was in it. Anyone who mattered, that is. Girls.

Bass guitar, that was Walt. Always the backup, never the lead. You'd think there'd be *one* oddball senior groupie who had a thing for back-up guitarists. But no, Walt Hightower was the only known member of a rock and roll band who attracted absolutely no attention from females old enough to drive.

Out front on vocals and lead guitar, Jamie Bingham had girls drooling all over him. True, Jamie never noticed any of them; he was so obsessed with his music, he hardly noticed his own mother. But that was probably part of his charm. Just because he was too busy for girls, they had all the time in the world for him. Walt's calendar was clear from now till the end of time. Seniors thought they were too old for him; younger girls seemed so . . . young.

Especially compared to Stacey. But here they were, together at last. Sort of. With Lee Whitaker out of town and nobody else willing to throw a big party, Nicole had come up with this First Night fever and he, Stacey, and Tiny had been available. Then Jamie had gotten Mushroom Cloud onto the program, and New Year's Eve had grown ripe with promise.

"Look at the crowd!" Nicole exclaimed suddenly.

Tiny was easing the wagon into a long line of traffic approaching the corner of Jefferson and Walnut. The street and sidewalks were alive with figures bundled up in winter coats and jackets, but plowing bravely toward the square. Children clung to their parents' gloved hands or skipped on ahead of them, scrambling over slushy piles of snow.

Colored light glowed ahead, where Walnut ran into the

square. It was a strange sight. This part of town was usually dark and deserted after 5 P.M., when the action was just beginning out at the mall. Even the handful of homeless people who drifted around the square during the day were gathered into the Mission Hotel by nightfall.

"Oh, wow," Stacey breathed. Her dark eyes flashed as they took in the streams of people on both sides of the street. "I don't believe this."

"There's Dawn Covington and her mom," Nicole cried. She rolled down her window. The pulsing of distant music rode in on a blast of frosty air. "Hi, Dawn! Hi, Mrs. Covington!"

The Covingtons waved and Dawn hopped over a blackened snowdrift to reach the Ford, stopped now in a backup of cars searching for parking spots. "Hi, guys!" she called through the window. "Isn't this wild? Everybody's here! Hurry up and park your car."

"Where?" Tiny asked. But the car ahead of him moved, waved on by a volunteer directing traffic into the First National Bank lot.

"Happy New Year!" Dawn called as the wagon inched forward. They chorused "Happy New Year" back, and Nicole hurriedly closed the window.

"I absolutely cannot believe this," Stacey said again, shaking her head in amazement. "Downtown Eli, the place to be on New Year's Eve! It's actually happening."

"I told you so," Nicole sang. "I know a great idea when I see one."

Walt imagined Stacey watching him perform in front of this amazing crowd, all of them—men, women, and children—crushed into the lobby of the state office building just to hear Mushroom Cloud. This was definitely shaping up as the night of his dreams.

He checked his watch again as Tiny maneuvered into a

tight spot in the packed lot. "I've got about forty-five minutes," he said.

Nicole retrieved a newspaper clipping from the glove compartment. "We have time for one other event before the band," she said, waving the scrap of paper at them. "Where do you want to go first? There's a whole list here: a string quartet, arts and crafts—"

"I'm hungry," Tiny announced.

"So what else is new?" Nicole ducked her head to consult her list by the glove compartment light. "There's a food court in the old five-and-dime building."

"That's been closed since I was a kid," Walt said.

Tiny sent a playful backhanded swipe toward Walt's nose. "Is that right, Lowtower? And are you a big boy now?"

Walt punched the air to the left of Tiny's grin.

"Children, children," Stacey interrupted. "Food court or boxing ring, make up your minds."

"Food court," Tiny decided without hesitation and led the way out of the car and onto the square.

Like everyone else walking in bunches for warmth, Tiny gathered Nicole under his arm, and she threw her own arm around the broad back of his jacket. Behind them, Walt sent another uncertain glance toward Stacey. She grinned and hooked elbows with him as she had before at her house, but this time with a happy little squeeze.

"They're in love," she said, nodding toward Nicole and Tiny. Her words popped out of her mouth in puffs of steam.

"Oh, come on," Walt protested. "They've been buddies since birth."

"They don't know it yet," Stacey said. "But they're in love. It's been happening all semester."

"Nah, they just joke around—"

"The jokes are changing. You mark my words."

Walt regarded the alleged lovebirds thoughtfully. Interesting that Stacey could detect microscopic changes in them and not see what was walking right beside her.

After the cold outside, the five-and-dime seemed overheated. In spite of extra lighting and a spattering of colorful First Night posters on the walls, the place still had a look of failure about it. But the holiday noise and bustle more than made up for the cracked ceiling and remnants of mangled shelving. Several local restaurants had set up booths along one wall. Tiny headed directly for the heavenly aroma of Smokey's Barbeque.

"This stuff is great," he announced.

Walt and Nicole got into line behind him while Stacey went to stake out one of the tables scattered around the cavernous room. Someone tapped on a microphone and called for attention. The roar of conversation settled down to a hum while a group of children in Scout uniforms arranged themselves on a platform at the far end of the building and launched into a program of folk songs from around the world. They were singing a round of "Frère Jacques" when Tiny's long arm finally maneuvered its way between two men with outbound barbeque platters and made contact with the counter.

Walt and Nicole squiggled up next to him. The girl behind the counter looked at them expectantly.

"Hi, Tara," Tiny said. "Happy New Year."

It took a moment for recognition to flicker in the girl's deep-set eyes. "Oh, hi," she said, and once again struck her waiting pose, pencil held ready above a grease-smeared order pad.

"I guess we'll have four combo platters," Tiny told her. "And a round of Cokes."

"Three," Walt broke in. "I'll nibble off yours. Or maybe

not. I'm beginning to feel a little queasy. It's thirty minutes till countdown."

"Three," Tiny said, "but you can double the sandwich and fries on mine. Walt's playing in a band tonight," he went on, watching Tara scribble in the corrections. "Mushroom Cloud."

Tara nodded absently and turned away to give in their order. Behind her, two men were slicing beef and frying potatoes on makeshift equipment.

"You know her?" Walt asked softly.

Tiny bent his large frame to answer. "She goes to Oakview," he said. "She's been in a couple of my classes."

"She's a senior?" Nicole asked.

Tiny nodded. "Yah, I think so. She doesn't ever say much. Kind of shy, I guess."

Walt watched as the tall, rawboned girl piled meat onto their sandwiches and scooped up mountains of fries. He was sure he'd never seen her before. "It's amazing," he said, "how you can be locked up in the same building with people, day after day, year after year, and never even notice them."

"Tiny knows everybody," Nicole said.

"Not as well as I'd like to," Tiny informed her.

As Walt watched, their eyes met and Nicole winked. Tiny was still smiling broadly as he turned away from her to pick up their platters. Walt shook his head. Stacey was right. And *he* apparently didn't even know the people he knew!

They found Stacey at a table near the Scout chorus. As the three of them slid into their seats and divided up a supply of napkins, the singers began to chant in what sounded like Chinese. A little girl in full Oriental costume stepped forward and sent long red and yellow streamers twirling through the air in intricate patterns. Then a dragon danced across the platform, six pairs of sneakered feet sticking out under its blue-green scales. The audience oohed and aahed their approval.

"We never got to do anything with the Boy Scouts when we were little," Nicole observed.

"We didn't have real Chinese kids in our troop when we sang foreign folk songs, either," Stacey pointed out. "Or black kids, or anybody. We were totally white bread and mayonnaise."

The troop's leader, a slender black woman draped in a white and gold robe and wearing a turban, played a final "It's a Small World, After All" on a rickety upright piano just below the platform. She bobbed her head and occasionally interrupted the melody line to wave the more bashful members of the troop forward for their bows.

"We had Sammy Weinstadt," Tiny said.

"Oh, right," Walt put in, "the only Jewish kid in our whole school until last year. We sang exactly one Chanukah song every Christmas, remember?"

"So Eli is finally growing up," Stacey observed. "Just like us!" Suddenly her smile faded and her face went taut. "Oh, no," she muttered. "Ah, nuts."

Walt swiveled in his chair to see what she was looking at. "What is it?"

"My parents."

"So?" Tiny asked. "All our folks are around here somewhere. It's New Year's Eve for them, too."

"Excuse me." Stacey slid her chair back from the table, slipped into her jacket, and hurried away, avoiding the food line where her parents were waiting.

Walt knocked over his own chair trying to catch her arm. "Stacey! Hey! Where are you going?"

He felt Tiny tugging on his sleeve and suddenly realized everyone around their table was staring—and no doubt thinking his New Year's Eve date had just run out on him.

Blushing, he righted the chair and then eyed his watch again without really reading it. "I better be going, too," he told Tiny and Nicole. "See you over at the gig, okay?"

They looked like a couple, all right, both of them now gazing up at him with all that concern and sympathy. It was painful to look at them.

"We'll be there," he heard Tiny call after him as he made his way through the jumble of tables. The Scouts were marching off the stage now, and everyone Walt passed was applauding wildly. What a nightmare!

By the time Nicole and Tiny arrived at the state office building, they were holding hands. Walt couldn't help but notice because the spacious lobby was practically empty, although the band was set up and ready to go. Oh, sure, a few kids from school were there—Dawn and her mom. Ian MacLaine, alone, as usual. That chubby one with all the makeup—Caroline—with her sidekick Brenda and some skinny guy with pimples. The inseparable Robbie Dougherty and Tanya Breuer.

The band's families lined themselves up proudly: the Hightowers, the Weinstadts, Jamie's mother. Not Dub's parents, of course, but nobody expected them, least of all Dub. Family outings were not their style. The band sure could have used two more live bodies on the receiving end.

Actually, one more live body would've made all the difference in the world. But Stacey never showed up. Her parents came, waved in by the Weinstadts, and a few other people wandered in, too, once the set got under way. Including Dub's uncle, an unexpected bonus. As usual, Jamie played and sang like a man possessed and

81

swept the band along with him. They couldn't help being disappointed by the slim attendance, but he didn't seem to care. Once the music started, Jamie just rode it. Eighty thousand screaming fans or a blank wall, it wouldn't much matter to him.

Or to Walt, really. But Stacey—that hurt.

As they took their bows, a man with a pockmarked face and a scraggly ponytail approached the platform.

"How old are you guys?" he asked Jamie.

"Dub's eighteen," Jamie told him. "Sam and I are nearly eighteen." He hesitated a second. "And Walt's sixteen. Why?"

"I manage the Cat's Cradle around the corner. I like your stuff. Look me up when you turn twenty-one."

He left, with Jamie gazing after him in wonder, as if he'd been Batman or the Lone Ranger. Then Jamie began slapping everyone's palms in celebration. "I told you guys," he crowed. "Didn't I tell you? We are *good*. You think you could skip a couple of years, Walt, the way you skipped fifth grade?"

"I'll work on it," Walt said ruefully.

He, Tiny, and Nicole helped load the band's equipment back into the Weinstadts' van, then strolled over to one of the bars, dry for the night, to listen to a jazz trio. When they came back outside, Stacey was waiting for them.

"Where in the world have you been?" Nicole asked her.

Stacey grinned sheepishly. "I freaked out," she said. "I'm sorry. I had a big fight with my parents tonight and I just couldn't be in the same room with them."

"That's why you didn't show up to hear the band play?" Tiny asked her. "Because you needed a break from your folks?"

"How do you think Walt feels about that?" Nicole added.

"Wait a second—" Walt broke in. He didn't need anyone standing up for him—certainly not against Stacey. But the three of them went on with their quarrel, ignoring him completely.

"I said I'm sorry, didn't I?" Stacey asked.

"That doesn't help Walt much now," Nicole persisted.

"Hey—" Walt tried again.

"What's the big deal with your parents anyway?" Tiny interrupted.

"I sent off my college applications this afternoon," Stacey explained. "To everywhere except Southwest State, which is the only place they think I should go."

Nicole groaned. "Oh, no, not that again."

"Yes, that again. The more I want to go out of state, the more they want me to stay. And the more they want me to stay, the more positive I am that I've got to get out. So I mailed three applications and took the one for Southwest State out with the trash."

Southwest State was less than an hour's drive from Eli. Many of the seniors headed for college would be there, Walt among them. But everyone knew Stacey had bigger plans: a theater major at Northwestern or Carnegie Tech or UCLA. Broadway. Or Hollywood. Or both. One summer at an East Coast theater had left her hopelessly stagestruck.

"You've been having this fight with your folks all semester," Nicole pointed out. "Couldn't you have laid it to rest for one evening? Walt and the band could have used a little more support from their so-called friends."

"Can I—?" Walt began again, but Stacey waved him off.

"Look," she told Nicole, "I've had a rotten day. My parents are trying to run my life, and I can't let them do it. So I don't need you making me feel guilty, okay? The band is going to survive without me. Walt will live through this. So back off, okay?"

"Could I get a word in here? *Please?*" Walt demanded, surprising himself with his volume. The other three turned toward him, mouths agape. "I do not need you people deciding what I can or cannot live through, all right? I am not a two-year-old, and I would like a chance to speak for myself."

The three of them lowered their eyes—and their voices. "Sorry, man," Tiny muttered.

"Thanks," Walt replied curtly. Now that he had their attention, he wasn't sure what he wanted to do with it. But the words came anyway—and aimed themselves directly at Stacey: "Yes, I am disappointed you didn't hear us play. Really hurt, as a matter of fact. And to tell you the truth, Stacey, I think it was pretty childish of you to take off like that just because your parents showed up. Is that how you plan to run your own life? By running away?"

The pain and fury on Stacey's face almost made Walt wish he'd kept his mouth shut. Almost, but not entirely.

"You have some nerve, Walt Hightower," she snapped at him. Then she turned and took off down the sidewalk.

This time Walt caught up with her. He grabbed her arm, but she shoved him away and kept on walking. He stayed beside her, dodging in and out of the steady stream of First Nighters passing by. Ironically, several of them wished him a happy new year. He kept his eyes on Stacey.

"You're doing it again," he told her. "You're running away. What are you running from?"

"You."

"No. That's a crock and you know it." This time he got a good grip on her arm and made her stop. She slumped against a newspaper vending machine in front of a boarded-up candy shop, head down, refusing to look at him. "I'm sorry I yelled at you," he told her, "but I was hurt and I guess I wanted to hurt you back. We're even, okay? But what else is eating at you?"

"I don't know," came the almost inaudible answer. "All of a sudden, I'm not sure about anything. Why am I carrying on like this—shouting at my parents, disappointing my friends, throwing out college applications, running away?" She looked up. "You're right about that part. I *am* running away."

"From what?"

Stacey pressed a mittened hand to her mouth. "Me, I think," she said at last.

"You?"

"What if I don't have any talent, Walt? What if I try to major in theater and I can't hack it?"

"Oh, sure, you can—" Walt said. How could Stacey not have talent? It was inconceivable. To him, anyway.

"Walt," she interrupted, "I've never even acted in a play, except for waving a trombone around in *Music Man* last summer. I want to be a part of that world more than I want to breathe, but I'm scared. I can't deny it anymore—having a dream and making it come true are two very different things. You know what I mean?"

"You bet," Walt said, but the irony was lost on Stacey.

"That's why I haven't auditioned for the little theater group here in town," she went on. "I tell myself it's because my parents don't want me out at rehearsals on school nights—and that's true, they don't—but I could talk them into it. If I really wanted to. If I had the guts.

"I didn't even try out for the school play. I got as far as the sign-up sheet and came up with all these excuses: senior year, I'll be too busy, and they're a bunch of amateurs anyway . . ."

Suddenly Walt felt a lot older than he had just a few

minutes ago. He wrapped both arms around Stacey and let her rest her head against his shoulder.

"I'm not ready for any of the schools I applied to," she murmured against his jacket. "That's all my parents have been trying to tell me, and in my heart of hearts, I know they're right. But I hate admitting it. I'm fighting to go away just because they want me to wait. What a mess! What am I going to do?"

"This is not such a big deal," Walt assured her. "Lots of kids take a year or two at Southwest to make up their minds about stuff like this. Then they move on. That's what I plan to do. You don't have to major in anything until you're a junior anyway. And Southwest has a pretty good theater program. I've seen them perform."

Stacey's head moved up and down in agreement. "You sound just like my mom and dad," she mumbled. "Only I don't mind it so much, coming from you. I could learn a lot in a year or two at Southwest. About acting. About myself."

And about me, Walt thought.

As if underscoring the possibility, a volley of fireworks crackled and popped out of the fountain at the center of the square. Stacey straightened up, and Tiny and Nicole appeared beside them, hand in hand.

"Friends?" Nicole asked.

Stacey smiled. "You bet."

"Time for 'Auld Lang Syne,' " Tiny said, and the four of them joined the gathering around the fountain to welcome in the new year.

The cold and damp didn't do much for the fireworks. But the entire square filled with people counting down the last minute of the old year was more impressive.

"Awesome," Walt murmured.

"Happy New Year!" someone shouted, cutting off the last few seconds.

Before Walt knew what was happening, Stacey had planted a quick kiss on his lips.

"Happy New Year, pal," she said. "I'll be right back."

She took off but didn't go very far. A few feet away in the crowd, she delivered greetings and a peck on the cheek to each of her parents. Then she was back beside Walt, turning him toward Nicole and Tiny—now caught in a kiss likely to bring on an early thaw.

"What did I tell you?" Stacey asked happily.

Oh, well, Walt thought. It was the first day of a brand-new year, and he still had plenty of time to play catch-up.

ERRORS IN SIMPLE ARITHMETIC

"What a relief!" Caroline Beck announced to the dirty white February sky. "I am so glad Student Council made the Sweetheart Dance a Ladies Pay All this year."

Brenda Phillips said nothing, just slogged along beside her friend, books clutched to her chest, head bent against the icy rain. She and Caroline had a two-block walk from the bus stop. They lived next door to each other and had been inseparable since their parents found them huddled together on Brenda's porch steps at the tender age of two, holding some sort of primitive conversation both sets of parents never tired of remembering and laughing about. After sixteen years, there wasn't much Caroline could say that Brenda didn't already know about, and that included her elation over the Ladies Pay All dance.

For the last five and a half months, since mid-August before their senior year at Oakview High School, Caroline had had something Brenda did not, something that had come between them. Caroline had a boyfriend.

And if Brenda now responded "Why?" to Caroline's "I am so glad," she would have to hear about that boyfriend. Again. Yet, what else could she say? Caroline had made her announcement loud and clear, face skyward so that raindrops quickly polka-dotted her thick glasses, and she was waiting, a half smile on her full, red lips, for Brenda to respond.

"Why?" Brenda said.

"Because George is absolutely flat broke," Caroline replied.

Brenda sighed, not too noticeably, she hoped. Slanting into the rain, she tried to think through the afternoon's calculus exam. There was something wrong with the third problem; she knew that. She'd known that the whole time she'd worked on it, but what was it? It was something obvious, and yet she couldn't place it. Behind the parade of numbers and symbols marching across her brain, Caroline's voice continued.

"Ever since he bought that stupid car, he's been pouring money into it. Why bother with gas and oil? I ask him. Why not just stuff dollar bills straight into the tank? We don't go anywhere anymore. We can't. The car's always in the shop, and he's an hour away, and practically all we ever get to do is talk on the phone.

"But now, car or no car, we will go to that dance. I mean, if the Student Council says 'Ladies Pay All,' ladies *have* to pay all, don't they? Even if it includes one of Eli's rare but reliable taxis to rescue my date from his dorm?"

They'd reached their side-by-side frame houses. "Guess so," Brenda said. "You coming in?" It was an unspoken rule between them that whoever said "You coming in?" first played hostess for the afternoon, if they had no other plans, which they rarely did.

They never stayed at school for club meetings or anything like that. "I'm not a joiner" was the way Brenda put it. "I have to baby-sit my sister," Caroline explained. But they both knew, although they never discussed it further, that they got out of school as fast as they could at the end of the day because it held little joy for them.

Not even George could help much there. He was in college, and he wouldn't have been an Oakview mover and shaker anyway. He'd come from some small blip on the Missouri map to attend Southwest State, an hour west of Eli. But first, he'd lived in town with his grandparents for the summer and worked at Angelino's Pizzeria at the mall. That's where Caroline had met him. "Love at first peeperoni," Brenda called it.

"Sure," Caroline said. "Let me leave my sister a note." In seconds she was back, trailing Brenda up the crumbling cement of her porch steps. "He can't say no, can he?" she went on. "I mean he can't make us stay home just out of stupid macho-mechanical pride, can he? 'Give me my Chevy or give me death'? Nah. And anyway, it could turn out to be one of the car's good days."

Brenda choked back a giggle and bent low over her key as it turned in the lock. George, macho? Homely, yes. Boring, yes. Macho? Never. George was tall and thin, with wiry hair that lay so close to the scalp above his high, oily forehead it looked like indoor–outdoor carpeting colored dead-mouse brown. George's large nose was spotted with blackheads; pimples rimmed his greasy-looking glasses. (Did they take their glasses off when they kissed? Did they kiss? Brenda shuddered at the thought.) George spoke in a humorless monotone. He wore khaki slacks every day and brown or tan polo shirts, long-sleeved in cold weather, short-sleeved in warm, that emphasized his skinny arms and sunken chest. George was primal ooze that had somehow learned to walk on its hind legs.

But George was a boyfriend.

"Are you going to ask anyone?" Caroline said, flopping onto Brenda's sofa. Her books hit the pillow beside her and scattered, half of them sliding to the floor.

"I don't know," Brenda said. She hung her coat in the front hall closet; plucked up Caroline's jacket from where it lay slipping off the arm of the sofa; hung that up, too; and made two neat piles of their books on an end table.

Her parents wouldn't be home from work for another two hours. That gave her an hour until she had to think about dinner. An hour to listen to what she already knew was coming from Caroline. She pulled off her wet sneakers, set them on the heat grate in a corner of the living room, and sank into her father's leather recliner, so old the springs in the seat made a dent perfectly contoured to incoming rear ends.

"You have to ask someone," Caroline said. "This is our senior year, Brenda. There won't be another Ladies Pay All. And you're going to need someone for the prom."

It was another unspoken rule between them that they did not directly address the fact that Brenda had never, not once in her entire life, had a date. Caroline had offered on numerous occasions to fix her up with one of George's friends, but Brenda had politely declined. She didn't want to hurt Caroline by mentioning it, but George didn't seem to have any friends. When he wasn't at school or in the pizzeria, he was watching TV in Caroline's living room. No one, male or female, other than Caroline was ever seen in his company.

Not that Brenda was any social butterfly herself. Class queen Lee Whitaker had nothing to fear from her short, limp, dishwater hair or her fat—buxom, full-figured, generous, matronly—body that had left the junior department in fifth grade and settled into a misses 14 by seventh.

Brenda gazed across the shabby room (her mother preferred "lived in") at her lifelong best friend—also large, also matronly at eighteen, but with long, now wet and stringy, brown hair. And yet, George loved her. And she loved George. Why? Brenda wondered—and suddenly realized that the mistake she'd made in problem three on the calculus exam was in the addition. *Addition!* Seven plus four was *not* ten! But on problem three it was ten, and it would stay ten forever, world without end. How could she miss something so easy? So *obvious?*

"Well? Are you?" Caroline wanted to know.

Brenda focused in on her friend's cold-reddened face. "I blew the calculus exam," she said.

"You didn't blow the calculus exam."

"I did. I added seven and four and got ten. That throws everything off. The whole problem is shot. Who knows what I added in the other problems? Six plus three is eight. Five plus five is four."

Caroline leaned forward. "You never blow the calculus exam, Brenda," she announced. "Maybe you should."

"What?"

"You are a grind," Caroline pressed on. "You have no fun. Ask someone to the Sweetheart Dance! I dare you!"

Brenda licked her lips. They tasted of Chap Stick, but they were still rough and dry. "I'll think about it," she said.

"All right!" Caroline yelped, shaking her fists over her head. "Way to go!"

Brenda lowered her eyes. She hated to see Caroline do stuff like that, pretending to be the all-American teenager she didn't even faintly resemble. Brenda accepted being an outsider, a creep, a nerd, whatever the cliques wanted to call her, but Caroline didn't. She spent hours mulling over the in crowd's latest news flash about who or what was in or out, entire weekends studying the latest fashion magazines, months dieting and gaining back everything she'd lost, searching for the look that would make her one of *them*.

"I said I'd think about it," Brenda reminded her. "I didn't say I'd do it."

And think about it she did: in line at the cafeteria, taking notes in calculus (where the dreaded exam had turned up an A–), regarding the clean-cut line of Brian Marsh's haircut as Mr. Ott droned on about liberty and law and scribbled predigested outlines across the board for the class to sop up and regurgitate on the next exam.

If she were to ask someone to the dance, she thought,

one gloomy afternoon in honors English as she drew little faces in her *o*'s while Mr. Barclay patiently answered somebody's dumb question, who would it be?

What about Mr. Barclay? He wasn't that much older— Don't be ridiculous.

It could be someone like Brian Marsh. Maybe his IQ wasn't quite in the triple digits, but he sometimes said hello and he looked and smelled good.

Who was she kidding? Brian Marsh wouldn't be caught dead at a dance with her. Not Brian, not Robbie Dougherty—not anyone remotely like them. They existed inside a charmed circle and didn't even know she was alive.

Fine. Forget them. She was better than that. She was above that. She'd ask someone nobody else would think to ask. She'd give some unknown quantity credit for full human status even if he didn't look like a movie star. She had brains; she'd go for brains.

On a wet Saturday afternoon, six days before the dance, alone in her parents' bedroom, Brenda dialed Ian Mac-Laine's number.

"Hullo?" a male voice said.

"Ian MacLaine, please," Brenda heard herself ask.

"Yuh?"

The pounding of Brenda's heart suddenly stopped. For a second, she wondered if she were dead, then realized the worst was over. She'd dialed; he'd answered; it was now just a matter of delivering the simple speech she'd prepared.

"Ian, this is Brenda Phillips. I sit next to you in Mrs. Redmon's calculus class."

"Yuh?"

Not exactly rampant enthusiasm, but Brenda pushed on. "So I was wondering if you'd like to go to the Sweetheart Dance with me. It's a Ladies Pay All, you know. The Student Council voted on that."

A long pause followed, on both ends of the line. Then Ian began to stutter: "Um—ah—er."

This was not a response Brenda had planned for. She had replies ready for "Yes" and "No," but stuttering caught her off guard. She waited, her mind a blank.

Suddenly, an odd sound, like a muffled crash, reached her from Ian's end of the line. "Ian—?"

"Can I call you back?" Ian said quickly.

"Sure!" Immediately, she hated herself for being so glad this nowhere answer wasn't a flat refusal. Ian meant nothing to her. The dance meant nothing to her. She'd resigned herself long ago to a life without dates. Some people lived without arms, legs, eyes, teeth—why should she care about *dates?*

Still, she hung around the phone for the rest of the afternoon and evening and stayed home all of Sunday, watching the rain turn to snow and praying for a blizzard so she wouldn't have to go to school on Monday and face him in class. Why had he said he would call her back if he had no intentions of doing it? This was worse than "No." A "No" could mean anything—he didn't want to go to the dance at all, or he was going with someone else. Even if he *did* want to go to the dance, but not with *her,* why make her wait to hear it? Why make her *care?*

She purposely avoided Caroline all weekend, hoping to surprise her with the announcement that she'd made the call and either succeeded or failed. "Don't ask," she said, the minute Caroline's face, a human question mark, appeared at her door Monday morning. "I called . . . someone. I have nothing to report. Just . . . don't . . . ask."

Caroline's lips, coated orange to match the flecks in her bulky brown sweater, opened and closed again. The two girls said nothing at all as they picked their way over the previous night's snow, far short of a blizzard but already packed into tread-marked ruts.

There was no stopping the bus from arriving and completing its usual trip to Oakview; there was no stopping the passing of time that eventually led to calculus. Brenda slipped into her seat early, opened her textbook, and forced herself to decode a new page of mysterious symbols. Even so, she knew when Ian arrived at his seat. His closeness made her skin crawl.

"I'm—ah—sorry I didn't call you back," he said. "Something came up. But I guess—I guess I can go to the dance with you."

Brenda's head snapped up. Immediately, Ian looked away, and she, too, lowered her eyes. "I'll pick you up at nine," he said. "What color's your dress?"

"I don't have a dress," Brenda blurted out. "I mean, not yet. But I like blue, so it'll probably be blue."

"Okay," Ian said. "I'll get flowers that go with blue."

"Thank you," Brenda said, but now his nose—his snub nose that he blew often into an old-fashioned white handkerchief—was buried in a textbook. It occurred to her that Caroline had said something about dinner out first. Everyone was going to that new Chinese restaurant.

Brenda tapped Ian on the shoulder. "Do you want to go out to dinner?" she asked. "Before the dance?"

"No, I can't," he said, his eyes red-rimmed and watery, as if he were battling allergies.

"Ladies pay all," Brenda offered.

"No. That's not it. I just can't. I'll see you at nine."

"Oh. Okay."

There was something wrong; she knew enough to see that. But, like the mistake in arithmetic on her exam, she couldn't put her finger on it. Maybe it wasn't important.

She'd aced the exam in spite of her mistake, throwing the class curve off, as usual. Even in an accelerated math class, she was a misfit. Even among the brightest kids in the school, brains were not what mattered. And whatever did matter, she didn't have.

"Ian MacLaine?" Caroline asked, on their way to the bus after school.

Brenda shot her an angry look. "Do you have a problem with that?" she snapped. After all these months of biting her tongue while Caroline raved on about George—

"No," Caroline assured her. "I just never would have thought of him. He's such a loner." Suddenly she giggled. "Remember when we were little and we used to pretend that big old house of his was haunted—and his dad was an evil wizard because he was so *old?* Boy, he must be *ancient* by now."

"I'd forgotten all about that," Brenda admitted and began to laugh. "We used to dare each other to ring the bell and get a peek inside. Maybe I'll finally get that peek, after all!"

"But first a dress," Caroline said. "I got mine at this great secondhand shop that just opened up on the square. Everybody's wearing vintage clothing, and Lucy's Yesteryear is *the* place to go."

Caroline took over the days before the dance, ushering Brenda through the dresses and accessories at Lucy's Yesteryear, fussing over her hair, turning the preparations into an extravaganza that Brenda had to admit was kind of fun.

And yet, uncertainty gnawed at her. Ian said nothing more about the dance when she saw him in class. In fact, he said nothing beyond "hello"—and that only if she said it first. Was he thinking about breaking the date? Was he planning to stand her up? When Friday finally came, she stopped him before he could bolt out of calculus as he usually did. "Nine o'clock?" she asked.

He nodded and was gone.

Caroline stopped by the house a little before seven with George to show off their outfits before they left for dinner. The gold satin and puffy netting of Caroline's dress made her look like a bloated Barbie doll, but she was so obviously pleased with herself, she was dazzling. George looked almost human in his preppy blazer and slacks. And his car was on its best behavior for the evening.

"Good luck," Caroline whispered, hugging Brenda at the door. "See you at the dance."

Two hours—two nerve-racking hours later—Brenda took the stairs carefully in satin pumps that pinched like crazy and an electric blue fifties cocktail dress that really made her suck in her gut not to burst the zipper. Her hair was brushed away from her face, the way Caroline had shown her, and a hint of makeup had been dabbed begrudgingly onto her eyelids, cheeks, and lips.

Her parents looked up from their places on the sofa and recliner and gasped.

"Oh, Brenda," her mother sighed.

"You look wonderful," her father said.

Without warning, tears tore at Brenda's throat. Was it happiness at the compliments? Or was it the sudden realization that her parents cared about her not being pretty? They'd never criticized her looks, not even her weight, while she knew Caroline's mother was always on her case about what she called one's personal presentation.

Neither of Brenda's parents had ever said a word, and yet here they were, beaming because she looked different from the way she'd looked every other minute of her life. She swallowed the tears and tried to bask in their approval. If a little eye shadow meant so much to them, fine; let them enjoy it.

Except it hurt, this pleasure they couldn't hide, pleasure that seemed far more heartfelt than the pride they'd always taken in her grades. People with a house full of cherished books, they were suddenly grinning and bashful because their daughter was wearing makeup and a secondhand cocktail dress. For ten long minutes, Brenda sat on the edge of a chair and watched them watching her in this new way.

At precisely nine o'clock, Ian MacLaine appeared at the front door, wearing a slightly outgrown navy blue suit and clutching a corsage of carnations sprayed yellow and blue. He said "Hello" with his face contorted as if he were in pain.

Brenda's mother's hands shook as she pinned the corsage to the thin shoulder strap of Brenda's dress, and her father sounded like a fool discussing the origin of Valentine's Day with Ian—lecturing him, really, since Ian didn't have much to offer on the subject.

Why were her parents so nervous? What was Ian or the dance to them? Why did any of this matter? Why were the smiles on their faces as they said goodbye at the door so hopeful? What on earth were they hoping for?

Ian held the car door open. That was nice. All the way to the school, though, the conversation consisted of her asking questions and him mumbling in response. She'd planned to ask questions—Caroline said boys liked to be asked about themselves—but Ian seemed reluctant to give out answers.

He worked at his father's law office after school, running errands. His mother was dead. He took calculus because his father said he should. He didn't much like math. He didn't much like law, but he guessed he'd go to law school. He didn't much like anything else any better. The house was not haunted, as far as he knew. He did not seem to find it funny that Brenda and Caroline used to think it was. Brenda decided to leave out the part about calling his father a wizard.

She had never felt such relief on reaching Oakview High School as she did this night, when whirling lights, hearts-and-lace decorations, and loud music relieved her of the need to ask Ian MacLaine any more questions.

A slow song began just as they walked into the gym, after leaving both their coats in Ian's locker, which was the closer of the two.

"Would you like to dance?" he asked. He was facing her but looking somewhere over her head as he said it.

"Yes, I would," Brenda replied.

Before the words were out of her mouth, Ian had her in a death grip. It struck her that this was her first dance with anyone who wasn't her father, Caroline, or a cousin she'd met at a wedding who'd carefully danced one dance with every unattached female over twelve. Ian smelled funny—not bad, just different, she decided. Sweat and shaving lotion, hair and wool.

He didn't dance well, but he wasn't awful. She could follow him more easily than she could Caroline, who'd done her best to prepare Brenda for the occasion. He didn't talk while he danced—Caroline never stopped chattering—but he held her so close there was nothing to talk to but his shoulder anyway.

"Thank you," he said, as the song came to an end, still not quite looking at her. He ushered her to an empty chair at the side of the gym. "Excuse me," he said and disappeared into the dimly lighted crowd.

Brenda supposed he had to go to the bathroom. Or maybe he was getting them something to drink. She smoothed the skirt of her dress and lifted the edge of her corsage for a sniff of the sweet carnations. The floor began to vibrate with a heavy rock beat, and bodies gyrated in front of her.

He didn't come back. Three songs later, he still hadn't come back. Caroline and George appeared at her side. Brenda couldn't help but notice the concern creasing Caroline's face, or the way she tapped George's arm and sent him off to the refreshment stand before lowering her gold-wrapped body into the seat beside Brenda.

"What happened to Ian?" she asked. "Why are you sitting here all alone?"

Brenda opened her mouth to respond but suddenly found it hard to breathe, let alone talk.

Caroline's eyes widened. She had a tiny smudge of mascara on her cheek. Brenda could have brushed it away but for some crazy reason didn't want to. "He did bring you to the dance, didn't he?" Caroline asked. "I've been looking all over for you, but I never expected to find you sitting here alone. And I haven't seen him at all."

"He brought me," Brenda managed to get out. "And we danced. Once. And then he said 'Excuse me,' and I haven't seen him since."

"I can't believe it," Caroline gasped. "Maybe he's sick. I'll send George to the boys' john to check."

George handed over the two paper cups of punch he'd brought, then spun on his heel, as ordered, and made his way back through the dancers.

"Don't ruin your evening over me," Brenda told Caroline.

"I will not let you sit here alone," Caroline insisted.

But I know how to be alone, Brenda thought. What she didn't know was how she could bear sitting on the sidelines at a dance with two people bravely keeping her company as if she were some sort of invalid.

"Let me handle it," she pleaded. "I'll be fine. He'll show up. Here comes George. Dance with him. Have a good time. Please."

George wore a guilty smirk on his face as he folded his skinny body into the chair on the other side of Brenda. "He was in the boys' locker room for a minute," he said, "but he's not there now." Brenda could smell alcohol on his breath. She must have made a face because he immediately pulled a stick of Dentyne out of his pocket and pushed it into his mouth. "There are some guys in there— with a couple of bottles of whiskey. They saw him come and go."

"You didn't tell them I sent you in there to look for him, did you?" Brenda asked.

"Well, you did, didn't you?" George said.

"No, I did not," Brenda protested. "Caroline did. Come on, you two, let me handle this, okay?"

George stood up, reaching across Brenda to yank Caroline out of her chair. "Fine with me," he said.

"*George!*" Caroline gasped.

"It's *okay*," Brenda insisted. Had she wandered into the middle of a nightmare? Would Ian never return? Would Caroline and George never leave? "Could you please go dance with each other? This is a dance, remember?"

Caroline hesitated for a moment, then followed George onto the dance floor. But they stayed close, too close. Caroline's concerned eye sought Brenda out too often, so she got up and made her way around the edges of the room, past the blaring speakers, to the refreshment table, where she spent several more songs nibbling pretzels and sipping punch.

When the parade of Sweetheart nominees and their escorts was announced, she managed to blend into the admiring circle around them. Finally, Nicole Drake was

declared the winner and led toward a throne of crepe paper roses by her date, Tiny Hurst, a gawky but kind of
sweet Prince Charming.

One step below them, other members of the Sweetheart
Court lined up for photos. Cassie Daniels was the only
one sobbing as if this were the Miss America pageant. But
she was moving away at the end of the month, so maybe
it did mean a lot to her.

Next to Cassie, Lee Whitaker smiled serenely. Accord-
ing to Caroline's Gossip Service, Lee was making the best
of a tough situation. Suddenly and madly in love, Nicole
and Tiny had become the obvious Sweetheart choices long
before the vote was held—especially since Lee had already won Homecoming Queen in the fall. Lee couldn't
take a chance on people denying her a second crown they
knew she wanted, so she'd campaigned like crazy for
Nicole.

Caroline said Lee didn't like Tiny much—and he'd
never been in a crowd of royalty before—but you couldn't
tell that now. Lee's smile appeared to be one of pure tri-
umph, knowing she'd backed the winner—and was pret-
tier than the winner—and knowing everyone else in the
room knew it, too. Leave it to Lee, Brenda thought, to turn
losing into an art form. Maybe Lee was faking it, but Tiny
and Nicole seemed to be a really happy couple, holding
hands and smiling up there. Beautiful, beautiful people.

After the ceremony, Brenda followed the ladies of the
court to the girls' room, where she fiddled with her hair
and makeup while they hugged each other and squealed
around her. She stayed at the mirror for several minutes
after they'd gone, looking at the face her parents had had
such high hopes for a couple of hours earlier, wondering
what she could say to them when they asked if she'd had
a nice time.

Finally, she went back out to the gym and circled the dancers to her original seat, on the odd chance that Ian would come looking for her there. The clock high on the wall behind the basketball goal said eleven-thirty. Her sentence was almost over. She was going to make it through. She was numb.

Then Caroline and George materialized again in the mass of bodies twisting and bobbing in front of her. Caroline smiled at her sadly and whispered something in George's ear. He glanced at Brenda, then quickly looked away.

It couldn't have been more obvious that they were talking about her if they'd seized the microphone and broadcast their conversation over the loudspeakers. Brenda knew exactly what they were saying: Caroline was telling George to ask her to dance so she wouldn't have to sit there alone through every single song, and George was saying he felt stupid doing it because it was so obvious, and anyway Brenda never liked him, so why would she feel better if she had to dance with him—and every other excuse he could think of.

All of which was true. Even though she knew Caroline just meant to be kind, Brenda couldn't stop an ugly feeling, a kind of fury, from sweeping over her. If there was anything that could thaw the numbness that was getting her through the evening and make her feel the full misery of her situation, it was pity from the likes of Caroline and George. Because let's face it, if there was anything lower on the social ladder than that ridiculous couple, that fat, gold-coated sausage and her pimply, carpet-haired boyfriend, it was someone who was being *pitied* by the two of them.

She hated their charity. She hated *them*.

And she hated herself. For being Brenda Phillips, born

loser. For choosing Ian MacLaine, not in honor of his brains, as she'd pretended, but because she'd figured his brains made him just like her, a nobody, and therefore the most she deserved.

No! It was even worse than that. She hated herself for knowing better and still judging herself and everyone else by Oakview High School brain-dead standards. She was no better than Caroline, adoring the in crowd that ignored her, or her own parents, gazing hopefully at their gussied-up daughter and wishing—oh, just this once!—for a beauty queen in the family.

Her head was beginning to throb. How could things that didn't matter at all matter so much?

The song ended, and sure enough, with a little shove from Caroline, George headed her way. Brenda stood up on shaky legs, revulsion filling her mouth with a bitter taste, her head already shaking "no." Bent on doing what Caroline asked of him, George received none of her signals.

"Would you—ah—like to—?" he asked, a bony hand reaching toward her.

"No!"

George backed off, turning awkwardly toward Caroline, whose mouth fell open in surprise.

"Last dance, everybody," a voice announced over the loudspeakers. And a body lurched past George and came to an unsteady halt in front of Brenda.

"Would you like to dance?" Ian asked, his words slurred and a stupid grin wriggling loosely around his face.

Brenda raised her arms and allowed herself to be jerked into position for the final, romantic slow dance. Ian reeked of alcohol and cigarettes and could barely shuffle his feet around the floor. And yet, Brenda felt herself relax in his arms. *Why?* Why was it better to be holding up a drunken idiot who had humiliated her than to sit on the sidelines alone? What kind of world was this she lived in?

The song ended. The lights came up. Ian swayed against her. "Let's go," he said.

George and Caroline rushed over. "We'll drive you home, Brenda," Caroline said. "We'll drive you both home. Ian can get his car tomorrow."

Brenda looked at Caroline, who was now gnawing her lip with concern. Caroline's hair was in wild strings from the dancing, she was practically exploding out of the top of her dress, and she was probably getting gold-frosted red lipstick all over her front teeth. What a mess.

"We'll be okay," Brenda said, aching to be home and alone. She threw her weight against Ian to start him toward his locker for their coats.

Wordless until they were out in the parking lot, Ian made one announcement before dropping to his knees beside a blackened mound of snow: "I'm going to be sick." And he was.

Caroline and George were right there to see it.

"That settles it," George announced. "Everybody into my car. Go on, you two. I'll grab the slob here."

Too stunned to resist, Brenda let Caroline put an arm around her and lead her away. George came up as they were settling into the front seat and managed to hoist Ian into the back. They drove the deserted night streets in silence. Brenda could hear the gentle shooshing sound of the tires on the wet pavement. She considered throwing herself under them. But she would have to get past Caroline on the one side or George on the other to do it.

Fat chance either one of them would let her.

At the MacLaine house, a Victorian hulk looming darkly behind gnarled, winter-bare branches, they discovered that

Ian had fallen asleep. He grunted and complained as George pulled him out of the car. The next thing Brenda knew, the two of them were scuffling on the sidewalk and Caroline was hoisting herself out the door and yelling at them to stop.

Brenda slid across the seat just as Ian shouted, "I don't need your help, okay? I don't need any of this!"

George was backing away from him, palms raised in front of his chest. "Hey, man, I was just going to see you to the door. No problem."

A light came on in a front room of the house.

"The wizard!" Caroline blurted out.

"Shhhh," Brenda warned her.

Ian turned his attention from George to the two girls. "What wizard?"

"It's nothing," Brenda tried to tell him. "It's a joke, an old joke."

"What wizard?" Ian demanded.

"That's what we used to call your dad," Caroline confessed. "When we were kids."

"When we thought your house was haunted," Brenda put in. "You know, I told you about that. We didn't mean anything by it."

Suddenly Ian started to laugh. It was a choking sound, more angry than amused. He began coughing and slumped back against the hood, bouncing the car. Brenda got out and stood close to Caroline.

"My father is no wizard," Ian said. "He's a drunk, has been since my mom died. But he's a lot smarter drunk than I am, I guess. He never drinks in public—and he keeps me handy to clean up after him. There's no telling what's waiting for me in there, but I guarantee you it won't be a joke."

For a moment, the night grew unbearably quiet, as if the cold air had frozen all sound around them.

"I don't understand," Brenda said, at last, "why you did this to me—to all of us—when you know how it feels."

"I was scared," Ian muttered, avoiding her accusing gaze.

"Of what? Of me?"

"Of you. Of me." He motioned toward the house with one hand. "Of everything."

It all came clear to Brenda then: their interrupted phone conversation and why he hadn't called back, his elusiveness before the dance, even his reputation as a loner and the red-rimmed eyes that were probably not caused by allergies. All her calculations had been wrong, every single one.

"There are people you can talk to," George said.

"I know," Ian agreed. "I've been—I've been working up to it. Or down to it."

"There's us," Caroline offered. "You can always talk to us—if you're not ready for the pros."

Ian actually managed a smile. "I better get inside. Thanks." He nodded shyly at Brenda. "Really. Thanks. And I'm sorry."

Brenda waved off the apology. "Forget it. I plan to. In fact, I think I already have."

The three of them climbed back into the car as Ian ran up the steps to his front door.

"The wizard," Caroline murmured.

"Yah," Brenda said. "Who knew?"

George turned the key in the ignition and the old car saw them safely home.

SPRING

THE BATTLE OF THE BANDS

"And *if* I go ah-wayyyyy—

"And if I *go*—

"And if I leave—

"But if I go—

"And if I ehhhh-verrrr go—

"And if—"

"How many more times are you going to play that line?" Jamie Bingham's mother stood in the doorway of his bedroom, wearing her weary-but-ever-patient look.

"I'm almost there, Mom. Hang in," Jamie told her, knowing full well that after this line of his new song, there'd be the next one to contend with, and the one after that. He let his fingers drift over the strings of his guitar in a pretty ripple and smiled encouragement at his mother.

"I've been hanging in for about twenty minutes now," she said. "I no longer care what happens *if* you go away. I'm looking forward to *when*."

"Ah!" Jamie gasped. "Mom, that's *it!* Thanks!" He struck the opening chords again. "And if *you* ehhhh-ver go away, the best of me will follow you," he crooned, then grinned up at his mother. "That's great, Mom!"

Mrs. Bingham sighed. "Jamie, it's a beautiful Saturday afternoon. It's spring. Don't you want to go outside? Just for a few minutes? You spend so much time alone in this room, I worry about you."

"I'm fine," Jamie assured her, but he'd already wandered out of the conversation.

The opening lines of his song were percolating in his brain, bubbling up one after another. It was like that, when a song really began to happen. It wasn't Jamie adding on words and chords. It was the song writing itself. Lines that had already been shaped in some cosmic other place came together in his head, as if they'd chosen him to write them down.

"And if you ehhhh-ver go away," he sang again, loving the sound, "the best of me will follow you. For all I am is what you see, and in your eyes is all of me—" The melody drifted off again, but Jamie relaxed, sure it would be back.

Ballads were not his usual style, but lately this one had been gnawing at him. He figured it had a lot to do with his senior year in high school coming to an end. This time next year, he'd be on his own—working on his music, his band, demo tapes, gigs—

"Whose eyes? Have you got a girl friend?"

—maybe even in his own place, with no mother standing in the doorway.

"No, Mom. It's just a song. A general goodbye kind of song."

"The daffodils are up in my garden," Mrs. Bingham went on. "The sun is shining. It's time to come out of your cave."

Fighting his way back to the melody in his head, Jamie nodded and waved her away. "Soon," he said. "Soon."

Mrs. Bingham took a step back, then hesitated before speaking again. "Your father called this morning. He was hoping you'd spend some time with him this weekend."

The melody evaporated. Jamie felt everything run down inside of him, like an engine with its power suddenly cut off. "I'm busy," he said, sorry his coolness had to be aimed at his mother instead of the person who deserved it but who wasn't there.

"Jamie, he is your father—"

"I'm busy." Pulling the red velvet-lined case across the rug with his bare toes, Jamie tucked his guitar inside and

111

stood up. "I've got to call the guys," he told his mother. "'Scuse me."

The forlorn expression on her face softened his anger. He grabbed her by the waist and right hand and boogied her into the hall to a chorus of "Proud Mary," then left her there, "rolling on the river" and shaking her head in exasperation while he headed down the hall to the kitchen to call his keyboard player, Sam Weinstadt.

Actually, Jamie suspected that his mother loved his music. She didn't like to admit it, probably because she thought he was close enough to neurotic obsession without her encouragement, and she worried that a year to try his wings might keep him from ever going to college. But he'd heard her on the phone, talking to his dad, who did *not* love his music: "Hank, he's not on drugs, is he? He's not in jail. He hasn't gotten anyone pregnant. He's passing all of his courses at school. There are worse things than dedicating your adolescent years to rock and roll."

Not exactly a rave review, but enough to keep Jamie's father at bay.

What his mon didn't know was that this was not a phase Jamie was going through. Rock and roll was in his blood; it was going to be his life. It already *was* his life. Whatever it took to get there—to the recordings, concerts, the whole schtick—he would get there.

He had talent, guts, determination—and a band that was really beginning to come together. The guys were finally jamming like the big boys instead of fooling around with it like kids. And their first major break was just a week away: Hooper's Music Store was sponsoring a Battle of the Bands right out in the middle of the mall on Saturday afternoon.

Everyone in Eli would be there. The Oakview High School prom committee was going to pick one of the bands for their senior prom. A paying gig. And not just the ten bucks a man they'd gotten at the Watering Hole's Teen Night, either. Real money.

More important, the prom would mean an entire night to do their stuff. No opening for anyone else, no sharing the stage with every pipsqueak ten-year-old who got a keyboard for Christmas. This wasn't the big time, but it was as big a time as they were likely to get in Eli, at least while they were still under twenty-one and couldn't play the clubs.

He dialed Sam's number.

"Hey, man, how's it going?"

"Oh, pretty good, I guess," came Sam's hesitant reply.

"You sure? You don't sound so good."

There was a long silence at the other end of the line. "I've—um—I was just getting around to calling you, Jamie," Sam said. "I had a little accident this morning."

"The van?"

"No. My sister's bike. I was showing her how to pop a wheelie, and I—well, I broke my wrist."

The news just didn't sink in at first. "Hey, that's too bad, Sam," Jamie said. "Are you in a cast?"

"Up to the elbow."

Jamie still didn't get it. "Yeah, but what about your fingers?" he asked. All Sam needed was fingers and a brain to play keyboard. Wrists and elbows didn't matter *that* much. Did they?

"Jamie, I can't play. I'm in this thing for at least six weeks. And after that, I'm going to be out of shape for a while."

Slowly Jamie saw the truth and realized he'd known it all along. He'd just refused to look it square in the face. "Sam," he breathed, around an ache in his gut. "Sammy, we play at the mall next Saturday."

"Can't do it, man."

"The prom is in two months. What about the prom? You'll be out of your cast long before that, right? You'll be okay."

"Jamie, it was an accident. A freak of nature. Well, actually, a freak of pollution. I hit an oil slick on the street. I'm sorry. I'm sick about it, I really am. I've been sitting by this phone for nearly an hour, wishing I didn't have to tell you, wishing I could undo the dumb thing I did. But there it is. You need a new keyboard player, pal."

Jamie slid his back down the kitchen wall until he was seated on the floor. "A wheelie," he said.

"The wheelie of doom," Sam pointed out. "There's a song in there somewhere, huh?"

"Yeah."

"You're not laughing, are you?"

"Not a whole lot, no."

Usually Sam could make Jamie laugh off just about any problem that came along. The two had been a team since the sixth-grade talent show, when they'd made total fools of themselves pretending to be the Stones. Undaunted, they'd talked Dub Colby and Walt Hightower into joining them, and the foursome became Mushroom Cloud, stars of basement, garage, and—occasionally—the school gym. Sam was the spirit that made it all such fun; Jamie was the motor, driving it forward. Together, they were unstoppable.

And Jamie had thought they really had it together now. They weren't kids anymore. It was time for serious moves, and they'd begun making them. They were ready to play their brains out—and now this.

Well, he wasn't going to let it throw him. Crap like this happened; you just had to slog through it. He wriggled back up the wall. "Okay, Sam, take it easy," he said. "I've got to find me a keyboard player. See you in school."

"Jamie?"

The voice caught Jamie just as he was about to hang up.

"Yeah?"

"It'll be temporary, won't it? I mean, whoever you find, it's only until I'm back in, right?"

This time Jamie had to laugh. "Go heal your bones, Weinstadt," he said. "Of course it's temporary."

"Okay, man. Thanks. See you."

Jamie replaced the receiver, then stared at it for a while. What now? Another keyboard player? Who? Where? Every player he knew was already connected with a band. But wait—

"Problem?" his mother asked, passing through the kitchen on her way out to fuss with her garden. March was too early to plant anything, but Jamie knew she had to get her hands dirty. Spring was calling.

"Nothing I can't handle," Jamie said. "I hope." He thumbed through the phone book frantically, then dialed again. His mother shrugged and continued on her way. "Tiny Hurst, please," he told the man's voice that answered. In a couple of minutes, Tiny was on the phone.

"Hurst! Jamie Bingham. You play keyboard, right?"

"I mess around a little, sure. Why?"

"I have this major problem," Jamie explained, and went into his tale of woe—the mall, the prom, the wheelie of doom. "We're rehearsing tonight," he finished up, "and every night this week. Can you do it?"

"Wow, Jamie, I don't know," Tiny said. "I just—well, I just fool around. I never figured on playing in a band. And I'm taking Nicole to the prom. We've only been dating a couple of months, you know? She might not want to spend her senior prom watching me play in the band."

"Nicole Drake!" Jamie yelped. "That's right! That's *great!* She's on the prom committee. That's a sure vote if

115

you're in the band. She'd *love* it, Tiny. Girls *always* love dating guys in the band. They're the envy of everybody in the room. Come on, it's not like a lifetime commitment. Sam's bound to heal up eventually. And then you and Nicole can reminisce for the rest of your lives about the time you played the prom."

"The prom's not a sure thing," Tiny pointed out. "The committee hasn't chosen anybody yet."

"Us, Hurst. They haven't chosen *us* yet," Jamie pressed on. "I'm telling you, all we have to do is show up at the mall and do our stuff."

"I know. I've heard you."

"See? You're going to enjoy being part of this outfit, Hurst. What do you say? You're in, right?"

Jamie pictured Tiny's huge, dark head bowed in thought. He was a giant, Tiny was, and he'd be a sight behind those keyboards. He was smart, too. And *serious.* Come on, Tiny. Come on, man. Do it, do it, do it.

"Well—okay."

"*All right!* Seven o'clock. Dub's house. Bring your gear."

By dinner, Jamie had called the rest of the band to tell them the news, called the music store to confirm their position on the program, called Dub back to tell him he had to bring his own drums to the mall on Saturday, and found out Dub's parents were going to be home and didn't want the band there. Dub's parents were *never* home—the band had come to count on that. Sometimes the Colbys disappeared for days on end, especially when the horses were running at Hot Springs. But tonight they'd decided to stay home. What rotten luck!

Jamie called the rest of the guys again and invited them to his own house for the rehearsal and then called Dub and Tiny back a couple of times each to arrange for Tiny to pick up Dub's drums in his station wagon.

The new song was on hold.

"What I play," he told his mother over a plateful of spaghetti, "is the telephone. Guitar is just a hobby. The telephone is my profession."

"Can't anyone else arrange things?" Mrs. Bingham asked.

"I guess they could if they wanted to," Jamie replied. "But I'm the only one who ever seems to want to."

Mrs. Bingham's face took on a worried look Jamie decided to ignore. His mom could find a lot to worry about, and more often than not, she was right. But her worrying never stopped bad things from happening—like his father walking out two years ago to join some twenty-three-year-old secretary on the road to paradise—so Jamie didn't see much point in getting involved with her concern too soon.

That didn't mean he could entirely avoid doing so. It was kind of weird that he was always the one getting the band together, scouting for gigs, writing the songs, calling rehearsals, reminding everyone to show up, practically carrying them from one location to the next. From the very beginning, whenever something went awry—which was often—the others turned and looked at him, like a trio of helpless kittens left by the side of the road.

No time to dwell on that now. "Got to get the basement set up," he told his mother. He planted a kiss on her head right where gray splashed the brown waves so like his own, and bolted from the table.

"Ugh! Did you get spaghetti sauce in my hair?" she cried.

Jamie hooted in response as he clattered down the basement stairs to shove the old paint cans and laundry baskets aside.

An hour later, Dub, Walt, and Tiny were there and wired for sound, and the rehearsal was going great. In fact, it was a miracle, a gift from the gods. Tiny fit right in. Nobody would actually come out and say it, but he added an energy level several notches above Sam's. Who would have thought the big lug had it in him? He looked like a bear, but he played like a mad dog.

At the end of the session, Jamie slapped backs and grinned like crazy as he helped the group maneuver their gear out the basement door and through the garage to the driveway. Even Dub, who never got excited about anything, seemed to be glowing, actually generating light as they moved around under the starlit sky, loading their cars.

"Dub's house tomorrow," Jamie reminded them. "And every night this week."

"You got it, man," Dub said, and paradiddled his sticks across the roof of Tiny's battered Ford wagon before jumping inside. "We are cooking!"

"We are, we are," Jamie called after him, shooting him an exuberant two-handed thumbs up.

As the week went on, Tiny's intensity grew, and it was inspirational. Dub's drums smoked at the end of his solos. Walt was doing things with the backup vocals and guitar no one had ever heard before. And all of Jamie's songs worked, growing and expanding as he bounced off the other three. Occasionally Jamie thought about finishing the new song, but there didn't seem to be room for a ballad just now. The tempo was undeniably upbeat.

Saturday's mall scene was a barely controlled riot. A makeshift stage had been erected in the main entrance courtyard in front of Penney's, with the names of the competing bands flashing on a computerized light board that hung from the ceiling. The courtyard and walkways leading to it were packed.

"Why is all of Eli in this mall on such a beautiful spring day?" Mrs. Bingham wondered aloud as she elbowed her way through the mob.

Jamie grinned. "Rock and roll," he said, dancing his eyebrows at her.

She returned his grin. "Well, I guess I'm here, too, aren't I?"

Mushroom Cloud was the third band up.

"Third time's the charm," Jamie told them. "Five! Six! Seven! Eight!"

True to their name, they exploded into their opening number, and the crowd responded with a roar of approval. They had fifteen minutes to show their stuff, four songs and maybe an encore if everything went well.

And did it ever! The sea of turned-up faces—crested with proud smiles from Sam, Nicole, and Mrs. Bingham—doubled their strength. Tiny was a maniac at the keyboard, shooting off sparks that electrified everything around him. Dub drummed his fingers to the bone. Walt wailed. Jamie levitated.

That was the only word to describe how he felt. The blood rushing through his body felt carbonated. His feet did not touch the ground. An encore? The crowd was ready to adopt them and take them home!

The last chord faded out over total craziness. Fighting just a touch of panic—there were so many people and they were pretty near out of control—Jamie waved the guys forward for a bow.

"Dynamite Dub Colby on the drum set," he shouted into the microphone. "On bass guitar, Walt 'the Kid' Hightower. And our incredibly special special guest, Keith Hurst—'the Tiny One'—on keyboards. I'm Jamie Bingham, and we are the one and only Mushroom Cloud. Thanks for listening."

119

They took the applause like pros: cool, but not too cool, a little strut to the step, a slight tilt to the head that said they knew what had happened here and it was okay. They could handle it, and they could do it again, any time they wanted to.

The man from Hooper's directing the contest finally hopped onto the stage and broke the spell, hurrying them off so the next band could set up. Nicole, Lee Whitaker, and Mr. Barclay, the prom sponsor, met them at the platform stairs with squeals, hugs, and a handshake. No commitment yet—there were other bands to hear—but the vibes were strong.

Behind the committee was Sam, right arm huge in its white cast, left hand ready to help with the gear. Jamie waved him aside. "Don't strain the little you have left," he quipped. Together they made their way through the crowd.

"It was perfecto, Jamie," Sam said. "Maybe I ought to break my wrist more often."

Jamie laughed and said, "Yeah, sure," but he found he couldn't look Sam in the eye. He knew Sam needed a compliment, reassurance that he was still in, still the best, but the words wouldn't come. The longer the silence went on, the more obvious it became that, given the choice between Sam and Tiny on keyboards, Jamie would have to choose Tiny. *For the good of the band.* Wasn't that the main thing, after all? Didn't the music always come first?

It seemed to take them forever to get to the mall doors. Out in the parking lot, the equipment hit the pavement and Dub, Tiny, and Walt yahooed and punched and smacked one another, Jamie, and even Sam, until they were winded and weak. Sam hung around for a while, a lopsided smile on his open, freckled face, then said he had to leave and disappeared back across the lot. Jamie still

120

couldn't think of anything to say to him. Nobody else noticed him go.

"I will never forget this experience," Tiny Hurst gasped, "never, *not ever*, not as long as I live."

Jamie rode Tiny's high out of his own slump. "It's the first of many, man," he said. "Stay tuned."

That night Jamie was on the phone again, calling the guys, arranging rehearsals, planning sets. He'd gotten a call from Lee Whitaker. They had the prom.

And less than two months to get ready for it. This wasn't a fifteen-minute sample, with six other bands ready to pick up the pieces if they blew it. This was three full forty-five-minute sets, nine till midnight, and it was the only senior prom the eighty-eighth graduating class of Oakview High School would ever know.

They met in Dub's basement Sunday night. "We'll have to mix some golden oldies with our own stuff," Jamie said, handing out lead sheets. "These are my choices. What do you think? I figure if we go, like, three hours a night and five or six on the weekends—"

"Three hours a night?" Tiny broke in. "For two months?"

"Seven weeks," Jamie told him. "Not a minute to waste."

"Jamie, Nicole and I just got together," Tiny protested. "This is very important to me. I don't want to mess it up. It's bad enough we'll just get to wave at each other at the prom, but if I never see her between now and then—"

"Nicole was on the committee that *chose* us," Jamie reminded him. "She'll understand."

"If I flunk out of school, I'm dead," Dub said, stirring behind his drums as if he'd suddenly awakened from a deep sleep. "My uncle says first he'll beat the crap out of me and then he'll throw me out without a dime to my name. Not that he's got so many dimes, but I always figured he'd take me on at the station full time after I got out of school. He says I flunk out, I can forget it. He doesn't need any more bums like my mom and dad in his life. And I'm flunking out. I need some time to hit the books, man."

"I can't believe what I'm hearing," Jamie said. "Weren't you the guys there beside me at the mall? Don't you know what we have here, what we could have even more of? We are at the beginning of something *enormous*. How can you even think about all this other junk?"

Jamie looked at Walt, expecting him to come in on his side and give the other two an argument.

"Not every night," Walt said. "I can't quit my job for this. My folks already have three kids in college. I have to pull my weight."

"Walt, if we're a hit at the prom, word is out all over town," Jamie insisted. "We could have gigs every weekend. You could make more in a couple of nights than you do all week at that library—and it'll be a lot more fun than shelving books. We'll be able to buy equipment—and make that demo tape Sam and I have been dreaming about since sixth grade."

Sam's name suddenly tasted bitter on his tongue, and Jamie fell silent.

Walt shot Dub a weird look, and Jamie knew something was wrong, wrong all around. "What's up?" he asked. "Come on, you guys, out with it. What's going on?"

Walt and Dub looked guilty as thieves. They'd been talking behind his back. When? Before the rehearsal? After Lee's call last night? Or even earlier than that?

"Those were sixth-grade daydreams, Jamie," Walt said. "We're graduating high school. It's time for real life."

"What are you talking about?" Jamie demanded. "Music isn't real life? What happened at the mall Saturday wasn't real life?"

Walt shook his head. "Maybe for you and Sammy," he said. "But not for—"

"Look, man," Jamie broke in, "if you don't want to be in this band, just say so. But don't tear it apart for the rest of us."

"There isn't any rest of us," Dub put in. "I want to go on playing, but not the way you do, Jamie. Neither does Walt, and Tiny just signed on until the prom."

Jamie looked from Walt to Tiny to Dub and back to Walt again. "I don't believe this," he said. "You're quitting on me. You're leaving me alone, with the prom committee to explain all this to?"

"We'll do the prom," Tiny said. "But we can't practice every night and weekends, too. We just can't."

"You want to give a half-assed performance?" Jamie asked. "You'll be happy with that?"

"It'll be good enough," Walt said. "This is the Oakview senior prom, not the Astrodome. We'll get by."

"Getting by is not good enough," Jamie insisted. A headache was pumping up behind his eyes. "Not for me. I want more than that."

"That's the whole point, isn't it?" Walt asked. "You're off on another planet lately, Jamie. We're leaving high school and you're leaving *Earth*. You're way out there, all by yourself."

"All by myself?" Jamie repeated.

Walt nodded. Nobody else said a word.

A lyric pulsed through Jamie's mind: "And if you ever go away . . ." He closed his eyes and rubbed at the pain around them. "So what do you want to do?"

"One week night," Dub said. "Tuesday is good for me."

"Couple of hours on Saturday or Sunday would be okay," Tiny chimed in. "But not both."

"Sunday, man," Dub said. "I gotta work at the station on Saturdays."

Jamie blinked a couple of times, then focused on the broken corner of a beige floor tile. "Walt?" he asked, not looking at him.

"Tuesday night and Sunday afternoon are okay with me."

"And after the prom?" Jamie asked.

"We'll have to see," Walt said. "But, Jamie, you might want to look around for a band that's already established. Or guys who are really—you know, into it, the way you are. Put up a sign in the music store, maybe? We have—other plans, you know. Work. College. Nicole."

Jamie ran the top of his sneaker along the break in the tile, crushing the edges.

"But it's been fun, man," Walt went on. "It's still fun. We'll be great at the prom—"

"It won't be the same," Jamie broke in, knowing there was no point in reminding them that the dream made all the difference. The prom was supposed to be a beginning; instead, it would be an end.

"No," Walt agreed, "it won't be the same."

In no mood to rehearse after that, the group agreed to try again on Tuesday, then gathered their gear.

Jamie sat in his car for a moment as the others roared off into the warm spring night and Dub went back inside the house. He rolled down his window and took deep breaths of the fresh air his mom was always raving about. It didn't do a thing for his headache.

He took a long time getting home, circling Truman Park a couple of times and driving figure eights in the Oakview parking lot. Tomorrow he'd put notices up in the music stores all over town. And he'd make a few calls. He knew guys in other bands; he'd check out the scene. And Sam wouldn't be in a cast forever.

Sam. After all this, what made him think he could count on Sam?

What made him think Sam could count on him?

In this world, it was a good bet that nobody could count on anybody.

Up in his room at last, Jamie took out his guitar and strummed the first few chords of his new song. Then he tried them again, in a minor key, giving up harmony for dissonance. There were too many goodbyes in his life, the chords said: his father; high school; the late, great Mushroom Cloud.

Forget that! *He still had his dreams.* The best of him was *not* going to follow anybody anywhere. That was sentimental hogwash. What he had—a howling guitar and a new song rising—was staying right here with him, and it was all he needed. Music was the one thing in the world he could rely on.

The notes built and built, one on top of the other. Sorrow transformed into anger; the song turned ugly, raced away from Jamie, out of control. Then it suddenly stopped short, its twisted, eerie tones blending and fading away.

Fingertips moving, Jamie experimented with a few more chords, but they just wouldn't kick in. The sound he wanted was out there; he could feel it, just beyond his reach. But something was wrong. After a while, he put the guitar down beside him on the bed and, elbows propped on knees, held his throbbing head in his hands.

He should've introduced Sammy with the band, it suddenly occurred to him. He should've called Sammy up onstage for a bow.

But he'd forgotten. No, he hadn't even thought about it once. Well, he'd been too excited. And, anyway, in all that ruckus, nobody'd actually heard what he was saying. No one was really listening to him.

Except Sammy.

Face it, Jamie told himself. There's more to it than the music. There's loyalty.

How could he have forgotten that?

Well, he was his father's son, wasn't he?

Of course, the poor jerk's secretary left him after six months for a hunk her own age. . . .

Jamie moved his guitar aside and stood up. His mother met him in the hall, on her way toward her bedroom with a bunch of daffodils in a glass vase.

"You okay?" she asked. "Those chords you were playing sounded painful."

"I will be," he assured her, then stopped at the end of the hallway to look back at her.

"Going to call your father?" she asked lightly, returning his gaze with a quizzical glance of her own.

"Yeah. Later. I will. I promise."

"You sure you're okay?"

Jamie nodded slowly. "It's amazing," he said, "how you just . . . keep things growing."

His mother smiled. "Tenacity," she explained. "It runs in our family. Tenacity—and a whole lot of talent."

Jamie doubled back and caught her in the old headlock hug. Holding her flowers out of reach with one hand, she poked him in the ribs with the other elbow and twisted out of the hold, laughing. For just a second, he circled her with both arms and she pressed her cheek against his. It was quick, and kind of awkward, but it was nice.

Then he moved on into the kitchen and dialed Sam's number without even thinking about it. His fingers had it memorized.

"Sammy?"

"Hey, man."

"I'm writing a ballad."

"No kidding, a ballad? That's news."

"Yeah. It just feels right, you know? Like maybe it's time to mellow out and think a few things through."

"Sounds good."

"Yeah?"

"Yeah."

"I'll play it for you, soon as it's ready."

"Sure. I'll listen."

"I know."

PERFECT

Today it did not matter.

Tara Owens pulled off her nightgown and folded it neatly while the sounds of her parents arguing downstairs in the kitchen tried to reach her, like the tendrils of something evil creeping out of the heat grate in the wooden floor of her bedroom.

The nightgown, a birthday present from her mother, was pink and as frilly as Tara's ridiculous *Gone with the Wind* name, also a gift from her mother. What kind of person, she often wondered, names her daughter after a plantation?

Tara tucked the gown away in her bureau drawer.

Her father had pounded on the back door before daylight—on his way to a new job, maybe, always a new job. Or on his way home from drinking.

It didn't matter.

It didn't even matter that her mother had let him in, actually opened the door and let him in—*again*—after all they'd been through: the slaps, the screams, the police cars, sirens blaring and flashers bleeding over their front yard in the dead of night. After all the neighbors' lights flicking on behind slyly fingered curtains and all the eyes peering out at them. The Owens couple, at it again.

And the ministers. And the social workers. The groups, the meetings, the hugs and hand-wringing and tears and confessions. Tara could not believe what people would tell absolute strangers who just happened to be seated in a circle with them.

After all of that, Lizzy Owens opened the door and let him in. Again.

"But it was pouring rain," Tara could imagine her

mother explaining. "I couldn't leave him out there in the rain, could I?"

No, Ma, you couldn't.

It didn't matter now.

Tara caught herself grinning at her own naked reflection in the bathroom mirror. There was a color in her cheeks she'd never seen before and a sparkle in her eyes. It was like knowing a joke and keeping it to herself because she wasn't ready to share it with anyone, wasn't quite finished giggling at it in private.

Her father could split open her mother's lip again; her mother could cry oceans after he left—more because of his going than because of her pain. The sight of her own long face, flat boobs, and bony hips could try to torment her, as usual. Today it did not matter. The secret was still hers to enjoy. The color and sparkle were within her.

Something crashed to the floor down in the kitchen and shattered. Larger than a glass, Tara thought, padding back to her bedroom. A water pitcher, maybe, the one her mother used now and then to tease the scraggly plants around the house. Just when they seemed about to die in peace, she'd remember them and soak the hard soil, splashing the floor around each pot. Then they'd revive, just barely, one green leaf among the brown, ever hopeful that this time Lizzy Owens really meant to do right by them.

Lizzy Owens had no business trying to keep other living things around the house. She couldn't even keep herself more than half alive most of the time. The parade of helping hands and do-gooders, the fellowship of recovering losers had taught her absolutely nothing. She smiled at them all wanly; nodded her frowsy blonde head; gazed at them through gentle, distracted, cow brown eyes; promised them anything they wanted to hear promised.

And then she went home and did everything wrong. Again.

She spent whole days in bed, sometimes, nursing her wounds, mental and physical, moaning for God only knew what. A life, maybe. Or an afterlife. She read her pocket-sized Bible enough to smudge its pages and her fingertips black. Why? Tara wondered. It never seemed to do her a shred of good. "The Lord helps those that help themselves," Tara had often observed. That explained His total lack of interest in Lizzy Owens.

Time was, Tara would have watered the plants, when she remembered and when she could find a moment peaceful and safe enough for watering plants. But no more. They were not her problem. If the police and ministers and social workers and groupies had done nothing else, they'd shown her a man and woman who would never do right by her or each other or anyone or any*thing*, no matter how often they promised, until they were ready.

And they might never be ready.

Until then—that nevertime—Tara was on her own. Maybe not out of the house yet, but out of its webs and traps and mazes. The plants were on their own, too. If they insisted on sending up their pathetic, groping, hopeful green shoots, that was their problem, not hers.

After the crash, there was quiet. Then the back door slammed and he was gone, busted muffler blasting off to the corner and away. Rain must've stopped. Anything left undone—or unbroken—he could see to another time. Lizzy would always let him in.

Tara pulled a black turtleneck jersey on over a green plaid skirt and went downstairs. Her mother was still in the kitchen, head buried in her arms on the table. She wasn't bleeding. She wasn't even crying.

On the floor at her feet, the pitcher lay in shards, its

thick base and handle the only identifiable parts remaining. Tara took a broom and dustpan out of the broom closet and swept up. When she'd dumped the last slivers of glass into the trash can beside the stove, her mother looked up.

"I'm sorry," she said.

"It doesn't matter," Tara told her and set about making instant coffee for them both.

Rummaging among the empty plastic wrappers stuffed into the metal breadbox on the counter, she found a white sack containing a pair of stale glazed doughnuts. She set them on the table on their crumpled waxed paper wrappers, next to the mugs of coffee, and sat down. Her mother leaned on one elbow and nibbled a doughnut absently.

Tara watched her out of the corner of her eye. How had she survived thirty-eight years, drifting as she did through time and space like a mote of dust in the air, with no more purpose or plan? Had she really married, borne a child, divorced, eaten, slept, and endured constant abuse without *noticing?* Was that possible?

That she barely noticed her own daughter, Tara could attest to for a fact, for as far back as she could remember. And it was more than buying frilly nightgowns for a decidedly unfrilly person. Years ago, strangers had come to the house and commented on the odor from Tara's diapers—when she'd been old enough to understand and be embarrassed.

By third grade, Tara was washing and ironing her own clothes, taking out the garbage, kneeling on a chair at the sink to clean up what few dishes they used. Meals were better eaten cold out of cans than half cooked or burned as her mother made them—when she made them, if that's what you could call plopping stuff on a plate, taking a few bites, and wandering off without a word.

What dream, what paradise, what other reality did those big cow eyes of hers see so vividly that its glare blinded her to everything here and now?

Doughnut and coffee done, Tara announced she had to get to school. Then she left the house, a bag of books slung over her shoulder. Her mother never looked up from the doughnut crumbs she was slowly rearranging on the table top.

Tossing the bag onto the seat of the creaky Dodge pickup some kind soul had given her mother—although Lizzy never drove—Tara folded her angular frame into the driver's seat and started the engine. It took at least five minutes for the contraption to warm up; it would just stall if she tried to back out of the driveway any sooner. She used the time to smear on some lipstick. Adjusting the rearview mirror, she caught sight of her eyes again. Narrow and green, like her father's. Thinly lashed. But still laughing.

Finally she put the truck in reverse and backed out. The potholed, puddled street bounced her along between its tract houses, perking up with forsythia and daffodils in the tentative April morning sun. Anytime now, the trees would leaf out and the redbuds and dogwoods would begin their early spring blush.

Suddenly delighted at the thought of it, Tara laughed out loud. In slightly more than one month, she would graduate from high school and get a full-time job and find herself an apartment and—

The daydream carried her all the way to Benton Road, where she joined the long line of cars blinking their left-turn signals to enter the Oakview High School lot. As the pickup lumbered across the gravel, she spotted Dub Colby leaning against his old VW bug, talking to a couple of other guys. The sight of him took her by surprise. She'd forgotten to think about him; on this amazing day of days, he hadn't even crossed her mind!

She parked where she could still see him and turned off the motor. For a moment, she thought about telling him. What would he say? What would he do? What did she *want* him to do?

A brief glimpse of happily-ever-after flickered across her mind—his smile, his arms closing around her. She shoved the image aside. She knew better. *Nothing.* That's what she wanted him to do. Absolutely nothing.

She grabbed her book bag, climbed out of the pickup, and locked the door. The group of boys never noticed her walking right by them. It didn't matter. Not today. She clenched her teeth to keep the laughter in.

Dub had done all the noticing he needed to do the night of the Ladies Pay All dance, two months ago. He'd turned up at Smokey's without a date, just as she was about to get off work.

"Hi, Dub," she'd said, amazed at her own nerve. She'd never have spoken to him at school. He'd squinted at her, caught off guard and confused. He didn't know she knew him, wasn't sure if he knew her. He had never noticed her, not at school and not even right now, standing behind the counter, pouring the last batch of potatoes into a basket for frying.

It was amazing how few people noticed her, anywhere, anytime. Her parents had always been too busy making each other miserable. Her teachers looked right through her, expecting nothing, getting nothing. Even the social work groupies had gravitated toward her mother, attracted to that dreamy helplessness, assuming, probably, that anyone as large and lean as Tara could fend for herself. Which she could.

She'd had a really good friend once—San Soomay, from

Cambodia. San Soomay and her family were refugees, brought to Eli by a church group who gave them a house to live in right next door to Tara's. San Soomay left town during fourth grade. Her parents said it was too hard being different in Eli. As soon as they had enough money, they moved to California to be with other Chinese Cambodians. There didn't seem much point in making friends after that.

But it was getting easier to be different in Eli. Look at Mr. Sanchez at Oakview, Tara thought.

Look at me.

"Tara Owens," she'd reminded Dub, running a damp towel over the counter in front of him. He'd nodded and ordered the combo platter and a Coke. "I'm in your earth science class."

A glimmer of recognition lighted Dub's unshaven face. "Oh, yeah, yeah."

Why she was bothering to talk to him at all, Tara had no idea. She filled his plate and set it on the counter, then stepped back and watched him dig in. He was kind of scary, really, always so gloomy looking. Maybe it was the dance going on at school and the two of them here, left out of it.

After the food, he still didn't say much, but he seemed reluctant to leave. "Wanna take in a movie or something?" he offered finally.

Tara wasn't sure she wanted to be alone with him, but said "Okay" anyway, before she'd thought it through. They waited out the last few minutes of her shift; then she followed his VW to the theater in her pickup.

The whole episode had seemed as unreal while it was happening as it did now, as she climbed the Oakview steps, remembering it. He'd barely spoken to her in the theater. She'd bought her own ticket, popcorn, and soda.

He hadn't objected—or eaten any popcorn when she'd offered.

After the movie, she'd followed him to the Lucky Clover Liquor Store and waited, freezing in the unheated pickup, while he stood out in the driveway, slapping his arms for warmth, cursing occasionally, and breathing steam like a dragon. It had taken four tries, but he'd finally talked a college kid into buying him a couple of six packs.

Then they'd gone to his house. It was a lot like her own—old, dreary, tired—except no one was home. Someone was always home at Tara's house: her mother. If Tara didn't drive her somewhere, Lizzy stayed put. Tara asked Dub where his folks were. He just shrugged.

Then he drank four beers to her one, hardly saying a word the whole time. He sat on the lopsided sofa, the six packs on the bare floor between his tan cowboy boots. She sat across the room in an itchy, sagging armchair, waiting for him to boil over like her father when the beer hit bottom and wondering how she'd get out of the house if he did and why she'd come in the first place.

Instead, he began to cry. Soundlessly. Tears slipped from under his eyelashes and ran down his cheeks, glimmering in the yellow light of the lamp on the table beside him. Never much of a crier herself, Tara still found his mood familiar. She'd cried like that when she knew no one would ever hear her. Her body went on making tears, it seemed, long after they could do her any good. Now and then, they just fell out, and she couldn't even think why.

For the first time all evening, Tara felt comfortable. She crossed the room and sat down beside Dub on the sofa. She touched his hand, wanting him to know she understood.

He never said a word, not before, not during, and not

after. When he was finished with her, he just stood up and left the room. She straightened her rumpled clothes, let herself out of the house, and drove home, wishing she could feel something. But she didn't know what to feel.

That Monday morning, in the hallway at school, she'd said "Hi, Dub" again, shyly, not knowing what kind of response to hope for or expect. He'd said "Hi" back and looked confused. He still didn't know who she was.

It didn't matter now.

Tara made her way down the hall to her first class. People called to each other and bumped into her as they hurried by. Outside her room, a couple was kissing, the boy's hands flat on the wall to either side of the girl's head. His body and arms formed a shelter to keep the world out—or her in.

Tara passed from one class to the next, feeling as if she could walk straight through the walls if she wanted to; she was that invisible. Her sneakered feet moved through the hallways, up and down stairs, in and out of rooms, without a sound. Her skirt swayed noiselessly against the long muscles of her legs. Behind the books embraced in her arms, her turtleneck pulled tight across her slightly swollen breasts. Her thin face smiled at no one in particular.

Only she knew the joke, the beautiful secret she held inside, the secret that had brought new color to her face and laughter to her eyes.

She was late. She had never been late before, had never had any reason to be late. But she was late now. She had skipped, actually, for the second month in a row. She'd gone to the drugstore and bought one of those tests, her heart racing as she slipped the box and her money across the counter toward the waiting clerk. An older man, he'd betrayed interest with just the slightest tilt of his head as his eyes met hers. She'd smiled at him, the joke already tickling the back of her throat.

It had taken her five days to work up the nerve to try it, five days of already knowing what it would tell her, five days of worrying that it could somehow deny the truth, change it, take it away.

Then early this morning, she'd done it. While her parents were downstairs screaming bloody murder, she'd thought, Oh, just get it over with, and slipped into the john and done it. And nothing, *nothing* else mattered now. She would be out of this school in just over a month, find a full-time job, rent an apartment—and have her baby.

All by herself.

That was the best part of the secret. That was the punch line to her joke: What she had now was hers and hers alone. This baby would be loved and would love her back. It would know her, notice her, care about her. She could already see its little face brightening at the sight of her, its baby arms reaching out for her every time she entered a room.

It would be a girl, a girl with a soft name, a pretty name, nothing as foolish as Tara.

Allison, maybe.

Or Michelle.

Laura. Yes! *Laura.*

And she would be perfect.

THE LAST RECESS

"By the time you get to graduation, you're too old for it," Stacey announced, as she tried to anchor Nicole's cap to her thick hair with extra bobby pins. "I mean, all this ceremony, these goofy outfits—who are we kidding? This isn't exactly the Supreme Court convening. It's Oakview High School."

"I think we look great," Nicole said, flipping Stacey's tassel until it hung straight forward off her mortar board and made her cross-eyed. "The guys scrubbed up, with their hair combed. Us in high heels."

Stacey shrugged. "Well, we made it, anyway. We're here."

"And we're supposed to be *there*," Nicole said, pointing toward the hallway. "Come on."

The two of them hurried out of the art room, where they'd donned their caps and gowns, to find places in the lineup of soon-to-be graduates. On the way, they stole a peek at the gym. There were huge bouquets of flowers everywhere, bound up in blue and gold ribbon. Gold posts formed an aisle between rows of folding chairs facing the school band in formal dress and a raised platform draped in blue and gold bunting. On the platform, more flowers, the school flag, the American flag, and more chairs awaited the graduates and their honored guests. Up in the bleachers, proud families in colorful spring clothes hummed and buzzed.

"Looks nice," Nicole breathed.

Stacey nodded. "Not too shabby," she had to admit.

She glanced up and down the two blue-robed lines of classmates hugging the walls across from the gym door and smiled at the faces she recognized. The boys were on the east, the girls on the west, as Oakview graduates had stood for the last eighty-seven years, fidgeting while they waited for the band to strike up their entrance music. The processional, it was called. Excitement tweaked at Stacey's stomach.

It was almost over. She was free—or would be in an hour or so. Free to make the dream of her life come true—a summer's apprenticeship at Lakeside Playhouse, then college and more days and nights onstage, learning her craft, loving every minute. Granted, she was only going to Southwest State for the first year or two, but it *was* the starting gate, and she'd be off and running. Oakview High School would be left behind in the dust.

Except for Nicole, sure, but that was *it*. And Walt. And Tiny. They'd always be friends. And Mr. Barclay, her all-time favorite English teacher, and Madame Stemmer—maybe Stacey would drop by now and then to say *"Bonjour!"* and see how they were getting along. . . .

What on earth was she thinking? Four years of her life, summers not included, she'd been trapped in this building, hog-tied and branded: High School Student. Enough was enough.

Well, she was nervous. Who wouldn't be? All those people watching her march across the gym. She could trip over her own feet. Worse yet, she could look at Nicole and get the giggles.

"Don't look at me."

"What?" Nicole asked.

"When we get in there, don't look at me or we'll start laughing and we won't be able to stop."

"I don't intend to laugh," Nicole said. "I intend to cry."

"Oh, you do not."

"Yes, I do."

"Over *this*? This . . . *junk heap?*"

139

"It may not be much, but it's the only junk heap I've ever known," Nicole replied. "Stacey, we've had some good times here. And there are people we'll probably never see again."

"Thank goodness."

"Easy for you to say. You know where you're going and why. You know what's coming next. I don't have a clue."

"You're going to KU—with your boyfriend," Stacey reminded her.

"Sure, but he's the only one I'll know there. Out of thousands of people, Tiny's the only one who'll know *me*. Besides, he's just like you: He has a plan. A goal. Exactly five years from this minute, he'll be an architect. And you'll be an actress. But what will I be? I feel like I'm sailing off the edge of the earth."

The band struck up the processional march. Stacey felt her insides lurch. All along the lines, heads snapped up, ties were straightened, fingers flew through already-perfect hair one last time. Nicole threw Stacey a helpless look and faced front.

One by one, the figures at the head of the line disappeared into the gym: Mrs. Cravens, the principal; Mr. Aramis, the vice principal; Ms. Tucker, the senior class counselor; Mr. Barclay, the yearbook adviser and prom sponsor.

Behind the adults Stacey knew were two somber-looking men in dark suits she'd never seen before. She would have guessed Secret Service, but Caroline Beck announced down the line that one was a minister and the other was a representative of the school board.

"It's illegal to pray in a public school," someone muttered.

"He's just going to talk to us," Caroline explained. "Not to God." Caroline always kept up with these things.

Last among the adults was the guest speaker, Anita Brock, the gorgeous new anchorwoman at Channel 10. She was paired up with the class valedictorian, Walt Hightower. Just before they entered the gym, she whispered something to him, and he grinned at her and blushed crimson. Nicole noticed it too and nudged Stacey with her elbow.

"Walt's falling for an older woman," she whispered.

"Shhhh!" Stacey hissed. "I'm warning you: Don't start me laughing."

"This is not a joke, Stacey Lawrence. This is our high school graduation."

"It's both."

The class officers were next into the gym: President Sam Weinstadt, Vice President Lee Whitaker, Secretary Tanya Breuer, and some drudge nobody knew who'd been treasurer. Finally, the ordinary, run-of-the-mill graduates shuffled up to the doorway, waited eight counts for the bodies ahead to launch themselves across the shiny wooden floor, then stepped out in time to the processional's insistent beat.

As Stacey reached the door, she found herself opposite Dub Colby, looking even more wretched in suit, tie, robe, and cap than he normally did in jeans, boots, and a T-shirt. Stacey had always thought of Dub as a total loser, but Tiny Hurst liked him, and Nicole loved Tiny, so maybe he was really okay underneath the permanent tough-guy sneer. She smiled at him politely as they marked off the distance to their rows together. Weird, she thought; we're classmates, we're marching toward our graduation together, and we're practically strangers.

When the entire eighty-eighth class had reached their assigned rows of folding chairs, Mrs. Cravens asked everyone in the bleachers to join them in standing for the

Pledge of Allegiance and the national anthem. The crowd of parents, grandparents, brothers, and sisters unfolded, sending a dizzying wave of color around three sides of the room. After they'd all pledged and sung and gotten seated again, the minister took entirely too long to tell everyone that education was a blessing to the young and the young were a blessing to the world and everything was a blessing to everything else.

As he turned to go back to his seat, someone on the boys' side of the aisle sneezed. A chorus of voices murmured, "Bless you," and nervous laughter rippled through the crowd. Stacey's eyes rolled sideways toward Nicole and found her peering back. Stacey swallowed hard to keep the laughter down and knew without looking at Nicole that she was doing the same.

Eighteen years old! They might as well still be eight. Stacey squeezed her lips tight and rolled her eyes toward the ceiling. The urge to laugh passed, for the moment.

Words poured down from the platform. Mrs. Cravens proclaimed that this was not a graduation ceremony, but a commencement ceremony. Their education, she explained, was not ending, but only beginning. Stacey turned her attention to finding her family in the bleachers.

The school board representative was offering greetings from his colleagues when she spotted her brother and sister-in-law waving and waved back. Her mom and dad were next to them, making silly faces at their year-old granddaughter. The representative didn't seem to know exactly which school he was visiting. At one point in his address, when he just couldn't refer to "your school" one more time without mentioning a name, he mumbled it as "Erghvew," just in case he'd guessed wrong.

Walt Hightower got up next and said a few words about the future and challenges and a lot of other corny

142

stuff in language so overripe most of the kids knew it was a put-on. He'd written another speech comparing high school to an endless nightmare, but Mrs. Cravens had suggested he consider something a bit more upbeat instead. Or else.

Sweet-faced and clear-voiced, he pulled off the parody without a hitch. But right at the end, he turned serious for just a minute. "For better or worse," he said, "we've touched one another's lives here, on purpose or accidentally, sometimes without even realizing it. We're getting out, but we'll never get completely away."

"Frightening thought," Stacey muttered.

"Or comforting," Nicole reminded her.

The evening's first genuine burst of applause blew Walt back from the podium to his seat. When he landed next to the anchorwoman, she smiled and his cheeks went flaming red again above his white collar and dark tie. It took a lot to shake up Walt Hightower, but Ms. Brock obviously had what it took.

Nicole coughed, but it could have been a chuckle. It struck Stacey as being a chuckle, and soon her own face was as red as Walt's—and Nicole's—as she fought to contain laughter that absolutely would not stay down.

"Don't *start!*" Nicole begged. "I have to go to the bathroom bad enough as it is."

That made it worse. That made it a lot worse. Stacey lowered her chin to the beige silk of her blouse and tried letting the laughter out in soft, measured amounts. "Hooooo, hooooo," she cooed, sounding like a lovesick pigeon.

It didn't help. Apparently, there wasn't a set portion of laughter that could be emptied in either one rush or a slow trickle. It was capable of reproducing itself in unlimited quantities.

Stacey tried the lip-biting, eyes-on-the-ceiling approach that had worked before. That was better. She really couldn't laugh with her eyes rolled up so far inside her head they hurt. In a moment, she was able to draw a breath that sputtered only slightly.

Mrs. Cravens was now introducing the guest speaker, Anita Brock. In the two months or so since she'd arrived in Eli, hers had become the best-known face in town. Not only did it grace thousands of screens every day at 6 and 10 P.M., but it smiled down from bulletin boards at busy intersections and rode the sides of buses all around town.

She'd taken Jason Daniels's place—Cassie's dad—when he'd moved up to an Indianapolis station. There'd been a farewell party for Cassie at Lee's house. Cassie had wept buckets, but nobody'd heard a word from her since. Stacey wondered how many of the kids around her would keep in touch with one another after tonight.

Anita Brock stepped up behind the podium, and a hush fell over the room as she sent her bulletin board smile around the folding chairs and up toward the beaming families. The class had voted overwhelmingly in favor of inviting her to speak at their graduation. The other suggestions—a local poet and a veterinarian—never even stood a chance. No one knew if she had any brains—she stumbled less than Mr. Daniels when she read from the teleprompter—but she was the closest thing Eli had to a star. A perfect choice for the occasion, Stacey thought, all pomp and no circumstance.

Ms. Brock tucked back a strand of hair that really wasn't out of place and began to speak: "I feel so honored to be here. . . ."

Her voice was softer than it seemed on TV. Huskier. Stacey had an urge to turn up the volume. But as the anchorwoman proceeded to review the story of her life—

beginning with her birth in Wichita—Stacey was content to leave her on low and just watch Walt Hightower salivate.

"Should've voted for the horse doctor," someone behind Stacey muttered, and a muffled explosion of snickers brought down a nasty glare from Mrs. Cravens.

Nicole moaned. "I'm not going to make it."

"Hold it in," Stacey whispered. "She's young. Her life story can't be that long."

It was neither long nor interesting, but enthusiastic applause greeted Anita Brock's final brilliant smile anyway, and then Mrs. Cravens took the podium again.

"Will the eighty-eighth graduating class of Oakview High School please rise?" she said.

Without the slightest warning, a lump filled Stacey's throat. She couldn't believe it. How could she possibly cry? What was there to cry about?

Well, she choked up at commercials, didn't she? Like when the soldier called home and his little old mom and dad were so touched? This had to be on that level— knee-jerk sentiment. There was no way on earth graduating from high school could produce genuine tears.

One by one, her classmates approached the podium to hand their name cards to Mr. Aramis, receive their diplomas from the school board official, and shake Mrs. Cravens's bony fingers. As Stacey waited her turn halfway back in the standing rows, she felt Nicole's hand slip into hers. It was cold. Stacey covered it with both of her own to warm it. When she turned toward Nicole, she found she couldn't see her. Her eyes were blurred by tears.

"Oh, this is stupid," she muttered. "This is unbelievably dumb. Those aren't even our real diplomas. They're just the covers. This is all for *show*."

Now her nose was running. And she'd left her tissues in her purse and her purse locked inside her locker. Their row was moving out into the side aisle. Nicole gave Stacey's hand a squeeze and took off toward the raised platform. Stacey sniffed loudly, reining in the tears and the drip as best she could.

As Nicole handed in her name card, Stacey began her march toward Mr. Aramis and the school board man and the moment she'd been waiting for all year. Somehow her feet got her where she needed to go; the rest of her apparently moved with them. The only thing from one end of the platform to the other that seemed solid and real was the silver filling glistening at the side of Mrs. Cravens's mouth as she congratulated Stacey.

"Thank you," Stacey murmured, clutching the leathery roughness of the diploma cover with one hand and Mrs. Cravens's fingertips with the other.

It was done. It was over. Moving away from Mrs. Cravens, Stacey suddenly had the feeling of stepping off a curb without realizing it was there. She stumbled, caught her balance, and continued back to her place beside Nicole.

"Are you okay?" Nicole whispered. "You look pale. You're not going to faint, are you?"

"I don't know," Stacey admitted. "I never thought it would be like this."

"Like what?"

Stacey shook her head, trying to clear it. "That it would matter," she stammered. "That all this—this stuff—would get to me."

Nicole grinned. "Told you so!"

Moments later, they were out in the hall again. Nicole made a mad dash for the girls' john, and Stacey went to her locker to get her purse and the tissues buried inside.

She waited there for Nicole, who fell into step beside her as they walked down the hall toward the principal's office to pick up their diplomas.

"The last time," Nicole said.

Stacey nodded. The weight of the rusty old combination lock clutched in her hand seemed to be the only thing keeping her grounded. What a strange night this was! She wanted to look at Nicole, to memorize her as she was right now, as she would never be again, but it seemed too painful to turn her head. The next thing she knew, she was sobbing in Nicole's arms. But it was okay. Nicole was sobbing, too. They hung on to each other as tightly as they could.

They finally said goodbye in the parking lot. In the morning, Stacey would be leaving for her summer apprenticeship in the Berkshires. By the time she got back, Nicole would be on her way to Kansas, to attend KU. They'd write and call, and they'd see each other on holidays, but it would never, ever be the same.

With a last quick hug, Nicole hurried away toward her parents' car. Tiny Hurst was waiting for her there. She slipped in close beside him, and he wrapped a protective arm around her shoulders.

Stacey had last seen her own family chatting with friends in the crowd lingering on the front lawn. As she looked around for them, her eyes caught the huge front doors of the school, standing wide open. Headlights from the parking lot flashed across the darkened classroom windows and highlighted faces in the crowd: Brian Marsh, Dawn Covington, Jamie Bingham ... What would they all do next? Where would they be a year from now? It seemed there was something she needed to tell them, but she couldn't think what, and anyway, it was too late now.

Stacey stopped looking for her family and just watched for a moment from the edge of the lot, remembering the first day she had climbed the broad stairs toward those doors, terrified, and the many days since that she had dragged herself inside or taken the steps two at a time—angry one minute, excited the next, frustrated, giddy, bored, eager, confused.

Nothing would ever be quite like this—this fortress, this fun house—where so much was held in and left out, where every word, every twitch, was bounced off a hundred mirrors and distorted, sometimes in weird and painful ways. She'd steeled herself against feeling anything but relief on leaving it, so why the hesitation?

Members of the school band paraded by, horns blatting sourly. The last thing they'd played, as the class left the gym, was called a recessional. Recess. The senior class had been dismissed for the last recess, the one from which they would never be called to come back inside. An image of her friends galloping across their elementary school playground, winter coats flapping and steamy breath shooting from their open mouths, flitted across Stacey's mind. What relief she had felt each time recess had been announced and she'd been catapulted out from behind her desk, out of the classroom door, out of the building, into the free, fresh air of the yard!

But there'd been an uneasiness even then. From the very first time, there'd been the disquiet of thoughts interrupted, projects abandoned, questions left unasked, unanswered. Out in the yard now, looking back at the gigantic brick buildings that loomed over her childhood, Stacey couldn't shake the feeling that she had accidentally left something important behind.

ABOUT THE AUTHOR

SANDY ASHER, novelist and playwright, is currently writer in residence at Drury College in Springfield, Missouri. She debuted with her first novel, *Summer Begins*, at Lodestar Books. After successfully publishing a number of young adult novels, among them *Just Like Jenny* and *Everything Is Not Enough*, the author returns once again to Lodestar with *Out of Here: A Senior Class Yearbook*. Of this book she says: "People often pass one another day after day, and sometimes they make connections and sometimes not." Two of the chapters of this novel have been performed as plays in New York City: "Blind Dating" at TADA! and "Perfect" at The Open Eye: New Stagings.

Ms. Asher and her husband are the parents of two grown children and live in Springfield, Missouri.